TARGET ELEVEN

(THE SPY GAME–BOOK 11)

JACK MARS

Jack Mars

Jack Mars is the USA Today bestselling author of the LUKE STONE thriller series, which includes seven books. He is also the author of the new FORGING OF LUKE STONE prequel series, comprising six books; of the AGENT ZERO spy thriller series, comprising twelve books; of the TROY STARK thriller series, comprising eight books; of the SPY GAME thriller series, comprising ten books; of the JAKE MERCER thriller series, comprising twenty books (and counting); of the TYLER WOLF thriller series, comprising seven books (and counting); and of the new LARA KING thriller series, comprising ten books (and counting).

Jack loves to hear from you, so please feel free to visit www.Jackmarsauthor.com to join the email list, receive a free book, receive free giveaways, connect on Facebook and Twitter, and stay in touch!

ISBN: 978-1-0943-8767-3

BOOKS BY JACK MARS

LARA KING THRILLER SERIES
ASSET ONE (Book #1)
ASSET TWO (Book #2)
ASSET THREE (Book #3)
ASSET FOUR (Book #4)
ASSET FIVE (Book #5)
ASSET SIX (Book #6)
ASSET SEVEN (Book #7)

TYLER WOLF THRILLER SERIES
DOUBLE AGENT (Book #1)
DOUBLE CROSS (Book #2)
DOUBLE ASSET (Book #3)
DOUBLE DOCTRINE (Book #4)
DOUBLE JEOPARDY (Book #5)
DOUBLE THREAT (Book #6)
DOUBLE TARGET (Book #7)

JAKE MERCER THRILLER SERIES
ABSOLUTE THREAT (Book #1)
ABSOLUTE DAMAGE (Book #2)
ABSOLUTE FORCE (Book #3)
ABSOLUTE PERIL (Book #4)
ABSOLUTE TREASON (Book #5)
ABSOLUTE VENGEANCE (Book #6)
ABSOLUTE TARGET (Book #7)

THE SPY GAME
TARGET ONE (Book #1)
TARGET TWO (Book #2)
TARGET THREE (Book #3)
TARGET FOUR (Book #4)
TARGET FIVE (Book #5)
TARGET SIX (Book #6)
TARGET SEVEN (Book #7)
TARGET EIGHT (Book #8)
TARGET NINE (Book #9)

TARGET TEN (Book #10)

TROY STARK THRILLER SERIES
ROGUE FORCE (Book #1)
ROGUE COMMAND (Book #2)
ROGUE TARGET (Book #3)
ROGUE MISSION (Book #4)
ROGUE SHOT (Book #5)
ROGUE STRIKE (Book #6)
ROGUE ORDER (Book #7)
ROGUE ATTACK (Book #8)

LUKE STONE THRILLER SERIES
ANY MEANS NECESSARY (Book #1)
OATH OF OFFICE (Book #2)
SITUATION ROOM (Book #3)
OPPOSE ANY FOE (Book #4)
PRESIDENT ELECT (Book #5)
OUR SACRED HONOR (Book #6)
HOUSE DIVIDED (Book #7)

FORGING OF LUKE STONE PREQUEL SERIES
PRIMARY TARGET (Book #1)
PRIMARY COMMAND (Book #2)
PRIMARY THREAT (Book #3)
PRIMARY GLORY (Book #4)
PRIMARY VALOR (Book #5)
PRIMARY DUTY (Book #6)

AN AGENT ZERO SPY THRILLER SERIES
AGENT ZERO (Book #1)
TARGET ZERO (Book #2)
HUNTING ZERO (Book #3)
TRAPPING ZERO (Book #4)
FILE ZERO (Book #5)
RECALL ZERO (Book #6)
ASSASSIN ZERO (Book #7)
DECOY ZERO (Book #8)
CHASING ZERO (Book #9)
VENGEANCE ZERO (Book #10)
ZERO ZERO (Book #11)

ABSOLUTE ZERO (Book #12)

PROLOGUE

The Royal Center for the Control of Diseases, on the outskirts of Amman, Jordan
Midnight

Private Jamal Obeidat was bored.

An eighteen-year-old from the small town of Safawi in the eastern desert, he had at first been excited to start his year of national service. Sure, it didn't pay well, and his lack of family connections meant he would never rise in the ranks, but at least he was going to be stationed in the capital where the movie theaters showed the latest films instead of ones from three months ago, and the streets were full of cafes and life. He'd even heard the girls were approachable.

Maybe all that was true. He wouldn't know. He wasn't stationed in Amman, but on the very fringe of the outskirts, guarding a disease research center, of all things.

He'd been here two months, ever since he had left basic training, and he hadn't seen anything of Amman.

The barracks for himself and the five other men who took shifts guarding this place stood right next to the large, modern research building. The two buildings were surrounded by a barbed wire fence with nothing beyond but dusty waste ground and a four-lane highway.

He had only had one weekend of leave so far, and he had spent that back in Safawi because his cousin got married.

So here he was, a small-town boy still dreaming of seeing the capital.

Dull. So terribly dull.

At least he wasn't on the border with Syria or Iraq fighting off Islamist attacks or hunting down gunrunners and drug smugglers. Two soldiers got killed on the Iraqi border just last month by a sniper. No one was sure if that was the smugglers getting their own back after that big bust last month or some Islamist with a grudge against a nation that allowed men to listen to rock music and women to walk the streets.

Private Jamal Obeidat believed in Allah and His laws, but those people were just crazy. Wasn't life hard enough? Why make it harder?

And cutting heads off the Christians was a sin. Obeidat had nothing against the Christians. The goalie for the Safawi Football Club was a Christian. Everyone called him "The Wall" because he never let shots past him.

Those Islamists would rather kill him than cheer him.

Obeidat shook his head as he paced the perimeter, causally looking across the open ground to make sure no intruders were coming.

Like any would. Who would want to break into this place? He supposed all that scientific equipment was valuable enough, but there were samples of all sorts of diseases here, everything from goat pox to bubonic plague to AIDS. The lab was part of an international effort by the WHO to study and stamp out common diseases in both animals and humans. You steal the wrong thing, and you could end up coughing up blood or getting warts somewhere you really didn't want them.

The place needed security, of course, but it would never be a target. That made Private Jamal Obeidat's job even more boring.

As he came around the corner to the front of the compound, he saw Sergeant Yazan al-Tamari, the commander of this little group of soldiers, checking the padlock on the metal gate.

"All's well, Jamal?"

"Yes, Yazan. Everything's quiet."

Yazan was a relaxed guy. He didn't go by military protocol unless a higher officer was around.

"Cigarette?" Yazan asked, holding out a pack of Cleopatras, a popular Egyptian brand. Jamal preferred Marlboros, but who could afford those on a private's salary?

"Thanks," Jamal said, taking one.

Just as Jamal cupped his hand to shelter Yazan's lighter, the roar of a powerful engine made them turn.

A dump truck was speeding up the access road from the highway toward the front gate of the disease research center.

For a second, Jama and Yazan stared at it in utter bafflement. Then Jamal cursed, his unlit cigarette falling from his mouth, as he unslung his AK-47 and flicked off the safety. Yazan got on his walkie-talkie and radioed to the others. Jamal hoped at least one of them was awake.

The truck sped up, heading straight for the gate. Jamal spotted a van about twenty meters behind it, using the truck as a shield.

An image flashed through the young man's mind, actually several images.

Of trucks just like this, ramming American compounds and blowing up. A favorite tactic of the fundamentalists.

Jamal let off a three-round burst that spiderwebbed the window but didn't stop the driver.

"It's armored behind the glass!" Yazan shouted as he fired full auto at the truck's engine block. Bullets sparked off the front with no effect.

The truck came right for the gate. Jamal sprinted to the right while Yazan ran to the left. Both men still fired, hoping beyond hope that one of their bullets would pierce the armor and do some damage.

The truck was almost to the gate. Jamal ran for the corner of the building with the horrible realization that he wasn't going to make it.

He winced as he heard a deafening crash behind him.

Shocked that he was still alive, he spun around and saw that instead of exploding, the truck had smashed through the gate, juddering as it dragged the crumpled remains under its twisted fender. Jamal raised his AK-47 and fired a burst at the driver's door. The truck wavered and screeched to a stop.

Had he hit the man?

He never got to know, because the next moment fire erupted from the windows of the van coming up right behind the truck.

Jamal cried out as a bullet pierced his hand. He dropped his weapon. Sergeant Yazan took a bullet to the head and dropped.

The front door to the research center burst open and his comrades rushed out in a disorganized mess, half dressed and still waking up.

They were easy prey for the gunmen pouring out of the van, who sprayed their tight-knit group with half a dozen assault rifles. Jamal gasped as he watched all his friends fall.

Jamal stood frozen, clutching his ruined hand as two of the gunmen approached him. They dressed all in black, with black headscarves that wrapped around the lower parts of their faces to disguise their features. Merciless eyes focused on him.

"I … I surrender!"

One leveled his gun at Jamal's head. The young man began to recite the Shahada, the Muslim testament of faith, knowing he was about to die.

The others rushed into the building.

"Put your hands in the air," the gunman commanded.

Jamal did as he was told. Blood from his hand dripped down his arm.

"Walk ahead of me," the gunman commanded. "I want you to show us around."

"I … I'm a good Muslim."

"If you were a good Muslim, you wouldn't wear the uniform of one of the West's allies. You are even worse than the unbelievers, because you turn against your own faith."

"No!"

Oh, Allah. Please don't let them cut my head off.

If they did, they'd be sure to film it and post it on the Internet. What if his mother saw?

"Move."

Jamal obeyed, having to step over the bodies of his friends to enter the research center.

They entered the front hall, passing darkened offices. There was a terrorist in each one of them, yanking the cables off the computers and carrying them out.

"Show us where the samples are held," the man pointing a gun at Jamal's back said.

Jamal was confused. There was a sign pointing to the main lab and cryogenic storage right on the wall.

Maybe these idiots can't read. And what do they want the samples for, anyway?

Stunned by the death of his friends, in agony from the hole through his hand, Jamal didn't even think of trying to fool them. Instead, he led the gunman meekly to the door to the main lab. Several of the other terrorists fell in behind them.

"I don't have the key," Jamal said. "The scientists take those with them at closing time."

One of the terrorists pushed him to the side and fired several shots at the lock. The sound echoed loudly in the corridor, jabbing the terrified soldier's ears.

The terrorist kicked the door and it opened. Flicking on the lights, the terrorists fanned out and began to grab every computer they saw.

The man who had captured Jamal, who seemed to be the leader, jabbed him in the small of the back with his gun. "The samples."

"This way."

Jamal led them to a thick door with a glass window on it rimmed with frost. Beyond, they could see a series of steel drawers. While it was freezing inside that room, the drawers were kept at an even colder temperature. One of the lab techs had explained that was to preserve the samples.

The leader nodded to two of his men, and they went in. Jamal stared as they pulled out lists from their pockets and began to read the labels on the drawers. One found a match and pulled it out, putting the test tubes into a cloth sack.

"Sir, these samples are highly toxic. If you let them warm up, they'll become active. The lab techs said—"

The leader clonked Jamal on the head with the barrel of his AK-47, making him flinch.

"Shut up. I don't care what those unbelievers say."

"But you and your men will—"

Another rap on the head. "Quiet! We yearn for martyrdom."

Jamal kept quiet. He was beginning to feel dizzy from the pain and loss of blood. His arm was soaked with it now. He felt sick to his stomach too. His arms felt like lead weights, but he didn't dare lower them.

After a couple of minutes, the two terrorists grabbed everything they wanted from the freezer. As they walked out, one put some bullets into the cooling system.

"That should make a nice mix of diseases by the time the security forces get here," their leader said with a smile. "When they come, tell them the Syrian Front for Jihad and Martyrdom has struck a blow for Allah."

"Y-you're letting me go?" Jamal could hardly believe it.

Their leader chuckled. "Go? Not exactly. You're staying right here."

Two terrorists grabbed his arms and dragged him, protesting and pleading to an office chair. There the two held him down while a third pulled out some duct tape and taped his arms and legs to the chair, winding the tape around and around his limbs to make secure bonds. Then they wheeled the chair to a spot right in front of the open door to the freezer.

Jamal gasped.

The terrorist leader patted him on the shoulder.

"If you have faith in Allah, you will not get sick. All power to Allah! Long live the Syrian Front for Jihad and Martyrdom!"

"God is great!" shouted the others.

Then they walked out, taking the samples with them.

Jamal stared at the freezer. The terrorists had opened every drawer even though they had only taken test tubes from a few of them. All the others remained.

Jamal looked at the thermometer and saw it steady rising.

Despite the cool air escaping from the broken refrigeration room, sweat beaded on the young man's forehead.

CHAPTER ONE

Trabzon, Turkey
That same night ...

Jana Peters was out of options, and she was almost out of light.

She lay on the floor next to her partner and lover, the CIA's top agent Jacob Snow, under a vaulted ceiling deep beneath a mountain. The tunnel to the surface had collapsed in an earthquake, and her entire belief system had collapsed with it.

Because that earthquake had been manmade.

She couldn't believe what she had seen with her own eyes, and yet she could no longer deny it.

They had been tracking down a series of thefts of rare medieval artifacts related to the Empire of Trebizond, the last vestige of the Byzantine Empire on the southern shores of the Black Sea. Their investigation led them to a strange cult that had learned to sing a special note through the crystals set in the various artifacts. This started a resonance that was just the right frequency to start a vibration in the tectonic fault lines that were so common beneath the Turkish soil.

In their fight to stop them, Jacob had been shot through the neck. While the wound hadn't been deep and had missed the spine, it had cut an artery, and Jacob had lost a huge amount of blood. Jana had managed to stop the bleeding, but he had almost bled out and was now lying unconscious next to her.

In a way, it didn't matter, because there was no chance of getting out of here.

When the cult had attacked, Jana had dragged Jacob into the underground chambers of a Mithraeum, a subterranean temple to the pagan god Mithras.

Most of it then collapsed in the earthquake. The main ritual chamber and the tunnel to the outside had fallen in, sealing off their only exit. A vaulted chamber deeper in the mountain had survived, but just barely. With the dim light of Jana's failing flashlight, she could see large cracks in the walls and ceiling.

There were two arched doorways in the chamber, both partially collapsed. One led to the main ritual chamber. There was no way out in that direction. The other led to a passageway going further into the mountain. She hadn't explored that yet. To access it, she would have to crawl over a bunch of rubble and squeeze between a couple of large, precariously balanced stones. If those stones shifted, she'd be pinned. If they didn't crush her outright, they'd hold her there as the air slowly ran out.

It was already getting stale.

Jana had to risk it.

She reached into Jacob's pocket, careful not to disturb or move him, and got his phone. It was the only other light source they had. Her phone's battery was dead, Jacob's flashlight had been lost in the quake, and her own flashlight was already beginning to flicker.

Jana also found a lighter. Another source of light but one that would consume precious oxygen. She took it as a last resort.

Touching Jacob gently on the shoulder, she whispered. "I'll try to come back. I won't let you … down."

She had almost said *die alone*.

Jana kissed him, moved over to the doorway, and shone her light in. The light didn't reach far. What she could see was a corridor half-filled with rubble, with deep cracks everywhere. It looked like it might be a bit clearer up ahead, but she couldn't tell for sure.

Even if it was, the tunnel was going in the wrong direction.

And this was a temple that had been hidden for centuries. Jana had found it only through careful observation. No one had looked down this corridor for a long, long time. To think that there was an exit there somewhere was foolish.

But it was her only hope.

She hoisted herself up onto a pile of rubble that came up to her chest, then had to squeeze beneath a sloped stone that didn't look too stable. As she wriggled through, Jana felt the stone shift, a trickle of dust running down her back. She tensed, ready to be crushed.

It did not fall. She got through to the other side, panting, looking all around her. The walls and ceiling looked like they'd collapse any second. Carefully she picked her way along the rubble, ankles twisting as some of the stones settled under her weight.

After about ten yards she got to a place where there was less rubble and the walls and ceiling looked a bit more secure. At least she could only put her fingers into the cracks instead of her entire arm. Her flashlight cast a faint glow down the tunnel. Darkness lay beyond.

Jana began to walk. The tunnel was narrow, barely wide enough for two people to walk abreast, and it had a low, arched ceiling that Jana did not trust. The Mithraeum had been burnt by an early Christian martyr, weakening the stone. The upper parts of the complex were blackened and already cracked even before the quake. The Christian, or more likely a whole crowd of them, must have piled up huge amounts of straw and wood to get such a hot blaze.

The Christians apparently hadn't burned this section. The walls weren't blacked or riven with old fissures, and so it had held up against the quake much better.

The quake …

Those cultists, a weird sect that wanted to revive the Byzantine Empire and kick out the Turks from Turkey, had found artifacts from the last years of that empire that had crystals on them that could resonate at a certain frequency. They had only sung for a minute, sustaining a single note through some trick of breathing, and the earth had begun to shake. The cultists had gathered at the medieval monastery on this mountain, built at the entrance to the old pagan temple, not realizing that the very martyr they honored had weakened the underground structure so much that the quake had shifted a huge amount of rock to crash down on them.

She supposed they were all dead.

But what they had done lived on in her memory, having changed her worldview forever.

For the past few missions, they had been chasing artifacts that supposedly came from an ancient civilization that had existed a hundred thousand years ago, a civilization of incredible technological achievement, one that had wiped itself out through civil war and the traces of which had been mostly erased during the Ice Age.

Jana and Jacob's previous mission had taken them to Nepal and Tibet, where they had come across artifacts that could cause an electromagnetic pulse that could take out electric systems for miles around. They had been housed in giant statues of the Buddha, and Jana had convinced herself that some modern mechanism was hidden inside.

But she couldn't deny what she had seen today. Or was it yesterday? Time meant nothing down here.

She had seen regular-looking people sing a certain note while holding aloft a medieval scepter and a medieval reliquary and the crystals on those artifacts had picked up that note, magnified it, and brought down the top of a mountain.

Impossible, and yet it had happened.

No natural crystal could do such a thing. Those crystals had to be manmade.

So Jana Peters, who had devoted her entire life to archaeology, had to come to the unavoidable conclusion in that dark underground passage that everything she thought she knew about the past was wrong.

There really had been a technological supercivilization, and some of its artifacts really had survived to the modern day.

Even worse, the Antiquities Division, a secret branch of the U.S. government, was planning to use these items to expand their own power. Its former employee Dr. Harlow had teamed up with the shadowy organization called The Order to assemble an arsenal of this ancient technology in a bid to rule the world.

And hardly anyone knew of any of this. Two of the people most likely to be able to thwart their plans were stuck in an underground temple that could collapse at any moment.

Like now. She came to a stop where a section of tunnel had shifted. Beyond a heap of rubble, the ceiling looked lower. Peering over the rubble, Jana saw the floor was lower too.

This entire part of the mountain had shifted. It was a miracle the tunnel had remained open.

Barely. And now her flashlight was noticeably dimming even more than before. The batteries were almost out.

Jana picked her way over the rubble. An ominous crackling came from the ceiling. She tried not to think of the massive weight of rock, the hundreds of feet of stone, dangling above her like the Sword of Damocles.

Just as she thought she had made it, she heard a loud crack above and behind her. She tried to leap forward, but it was too late. A stone struck her in the back, throwing her face first onto a sliding slope of stone. The air filled with dust and she was driven several feet down the corridor, stones striking her from above.

And then everything subsided. Nothing more came from the ceiling except the crackling of stone readjusting its weight, ready at any moment to come crashing down and squash her like a bug.

She had to move. Jana pulled herself up painfully, her back and shoulders aching in several places.

The tunnel had been plunged into darkness. She had lost her flashlight and it must have been crushed by the cave in. The dust hanging in the air gave her a sudden coughing fit. She swore that as she coughed, the crackling of the ceiling got louder. She clamped a hand over her nose and mouth and tried to stop. After several silent coughs, her body tensing with each and making her fresh bruises sing with pain, she managed to control herself.

She reached into her pocket for Jacob's phone and felt the raw edge of panic when she didn't find it. Jana felt for the light and let out a gasp of relief to find it was still there.

Jana flicked on the lighter and peered around. Dust hung heavy in the air, scratching her throat and tickling her nostrils. She resisted the urge to sneeze and cough. She found herself lying on a slope of rubble that was bigger than what she remembered. Looking over her shoulder the way she had come, she felt a rush of relief to see that the tunnel wasn't blocked. The rubble that had fallen from the ceiling had tumbled down into the lower portion of the split tunnel and the space she had passed through was no smaller than before.

Then she looked at the ceiling, and her heart clenched.

Deep cracks ran as far as her little light would shine, and directly above her hung a giant spike of stone barely held up by cracked rocks in two places. It looked like it would come down with nothing more than a slap of the hand.

Jana eased her way down the slope of rubble to get out of the way of the stone spike. Once she got a few feet, she hurried down the rest of the rubble and into the corridor.

She stood, panting with fear and exertion. Then she cursed as the lighter burned her finger. Jana let it go out and stood in the utter darkness for a minute, trying to recover. Hard to do when you're lost and can't see anything.

Then she lit the lighter again. Peering back at the cave-in, she spotted a gleam among the rocks. She stepped forward and saw it was Jacob's phone, shattered by a falling stone.

So I'm down to a single lighter, she thought. She let it go out and shook it. Half full.

Great. Just great.

Jana turned and felt her way along the corridor, extending both hands to trail her fingers along the wall. Once she stumbled on a rock, but mostly the way was clear. It seemed like the corridor sloped downwards. After a minute, her right hand felt nothing but air.

She flicked on the lighter and saw a side chamber. Stepping inside, she discovered Roman-era frescoes, the colors still bright thanks to being sheltered from the elements all these years. They portrayed Mithras, the Persian god who had become popular in the last years of paganism, stabbing a bull in the neck, a sacrifice to bring wisdom to mankind. Flanking him were Cautes and Cautopates, twin torchbearers, one holding his torch aloft, the other holding it facing the ground. The meaning of this symbolism was obscure and archaeologists had argued about them for generations. One convincing theory was that it had something to do with the rise and fall of the seasons.

On other walls were images of men reclining on couches while eating and drinking wine, the sacred feast of the followers of Mithras. Some of the men had names written in Latin and Greek next to them, most likely local leaders who had donated the money to build this underground network.

An amazing discovery, but it didn't get her any closer to saving her own and Jacob's lives. She turned away and went back down the corridor.

Again, she let the lighter go out to save its precious fluid. She ran her fingers along the wall, probing with her feet ahead of her to keep from tripping over any rubble.

It was good that she did, because after another few minutes her toe pushed beyond the level of the floor to an unknown space beyond.

She froze. Was that a soft breeze she felt on her face? And what was that sound that came so faintly to her ears?

Jana took a step back and flicked on the lighter.

She saw another break in the corridor, far bigger this time. The floor had given way into what looked like a natural cave.

Jana knelt down and peeked below. She could see a steep slope of loose rock leading down, and just at the edge of her vision a small stream.

This must be a natural cave at the foot of the mountain. Maybe there was a secret exit from the temple here. It would make sense since many rituals for Mithras were held in caves. The quake broke off the end of this tunnel and opened it right up.

She positioned herself at what looked like the easiest spot to climb down and let her lighter go out.

The climb would take both hands. That meant she had to do it in the dark.

She turned, got on her belly, and felt out with her feet. The first stone she put her weight on broke free, setting off a cascade of rocks to tumble into the darkness beneath her. Luckily, most of her upper body was still on the floor of the tunnel so, she didn't fall. The sound of falling stones echoed in the large, unexplored space below.

Then she found firmer footing and began to work her way down, testing every foothold and handhold.

Jana's head began to throb from the stress and effort. A bullet had grazed her skull a few days before, and she thought she was still suffering the effects of a concussion.

She should be in bed. The mission hadn't allowed for that.

Another foothold. Another handhold. For every firm spot, she had to reject several others that felt too loose.

Slowly, painfully, she made progress. Her head throbbed and she felt dizzy, so Jana forced herself to go slow and take even breaths. She should be down soon.

Just as she thought that, a foothold that had felt firm broke off under her weight. The sudden jerk of her body made one of her handholds break off too.

Jana felt herself falling into the darkness.

The terror only lasted a moment. She hit rock, her ankle twisted with a sharp pain, and she fell to the side.

She just managed to get her hands out to block her fall, scraping them but at least stopping any impact to her head.

Her body thudded onto rough stones, knocking the air out of her.

She lay for a minute, panting and sore all over.

Gingerly she tried turning her ankle and got rewarded with a lot more pain. A bad sprain. Probably not broken, but she sure wasn't going to be walking on it.

Then something caught her eye.

The faint glow of daylight.

Daylight? Yes! Several yards away, she could see the outline of a crack big enough to get through. It must lead to the surface!

Jana began to crawl over the rough stones.

CHAPTER TWO

Athens, Greece
One week later ...

Jacob Snow was feeling much better. As in alive. Alive was always the better option.

He didn't remember the Turkish rescue team digging him out of that underground temple, and he didn't remember being airlifted to a hospital in Greece. He also didn't remember the gallons of blood they had pumped into him or the stitches they had to put on his neck.

What he did remember was waking up in the hospital a couple of days later to see Tyler Wallace and Jana sitting on either side of his bed.

He also remembered his newly found consciousness being greeted by a long, luxuriant kiss.

From Jana, not Tyler. Jacob's boss was old school that way.

Jana hadn't suffered anything more than a sprained ankle and a few bruises from a fall while finding a way out of the ancient underground temple. It was painful to walk and the Greek doctors had given her crutches. Not a bad deal, because that meant she stayed by his bedside and gave him more kisses.

Now it was a week after he had been saved, and both of them were recovered. More or less.

They were still bruised and battered, still had bandages in various places, but at least Jana could walk again just fine.

He still worried about that head injury. The Greeks said her concussion was still healing and she should take it easy. Jana claimed she didn't feel any symptoms anymore.

He was doing better, too. While that neck wound had snipped an artery, it wasn't all that deep and a few stitches and a week's rest was all he needed to feel fighting fit.

Jacob Snow had always been a quick healer. He needed it in this job.

Now Tyler Wallace had summoned them to a private meeting spot to talk about the most recent events. He had kept them in the dark for a whole week, letting their minds rest as well as their bodies.

Jacob had felt grateful for the break. It had given him the courage to tell Tyler, who had for years been both a boss and a friend, that he had come to a decision.

He was quitting the CIA. Jana had nearly been killed on this last mission. Maybe if he quit, she would quit too.

Even if she didn't, he couldn't take it anymore. Jacob Snow wanted a real life. He wanted to spend time on his sailboat in the Aegean. He wanted to walk into a bar without scanning everyone in the room and looking for escape routes. He wanted to go to the supermarket unarmed.

It had been so long since he had lived a life like that, he wasn't sure what it was like. All he knew was that he wanted it.

He'd tell his boss as soon as he saw him.

Tyler had picked a meeting place so secret that even Jacob hadn't known about it until a year ago when they needed it as a refuge. It stood not far from Jacob's old home to the east of Athens, a disused windmill high on a hill. The blades had been removed, and an outbuilding had been added. The whole thing was whitewashed and shone in the Mediterranean sun.

It was the home of Tyler's Greek girlfriend. Another secret Jacob hadn't known. He probably would have never known if they hadn't been on the run with Tyler wounded and needed to go to the nearest safe place.

Jacob drove up the long gravel road to the hilltop and saw the door to the windmill open. An attractive Greek woman in her middle age came out and shot them a venomous look. He had gotten that look from the lovers of a lot of CIA agents.

Tyler's car was already parked next to the windmill. Poor Tyler. He had probably gotten an earful.

Jacob parked, and they got out. He put on his most winning smile and said in Greek, "Good to see you again. We were never properly introduced. I'm—"

"I don't want to know your name," she snapped. "Or hers. And you don't get to know mine."

"Okay."

"You get to meet at my house because there's no safer place. Come inside."

Despite her foul mood, she hadn't skimped on traditional Greek hospitality. The ground floor was one large circular room with an open kitchen to one side, a lounge area, and the rest given over to an old oak table covered in snacks—olives, dolmehs, bread, a salad, a bottle of wine and another of ouzo, and water for those who needed to keep their head straight for whatever Tyler was about to lay on them.

Tyler Wallace himself sat at the head of the table. A far better position than his last visit, when he had been laid out on the table and bleeding all over it. Tyler's unnamed girlfriend was a surgeon and had patched him up, then cooked them a delicious meal, all the while cursing Jacob and Jana's lineage back ten generations.

"Hello, Agent Snow and Agent Peters. How are you feeling?"

Like I'm ready to quit.

"Fully recovered, sir," Jacob replied. He'd get to his resignation in a minute. To his surprise, he didn't feel nervous. It was the right time.

"I'm fine too," Jana said. "The ankle is good and my hair is growing back."

Jacob nudged her. "Not enough that you feel comfortable taking off your hat even when you're indoors."

"Hey, I'm a girl."

"You're way more than that. I'm a lucky man. You're a lucky man, too, sir."

Jacob looked around, hoping the sour surgeon had overheard, but she had made herself scarce.

"Is my father coming?" Jana asked.

"We'll get to him in a moment," their boss said.

Tyler Wallace leaned on the table, folding his hands.

"Let me get you up to speed. We discovered that Arnold Drake, the head of the CIA office in Ankara, was with The Order. He convinced Ahmet Balik that you two were actually with that organization. He was fooled, an innocent victim. Sadly, he's dead."

Jacob bowed his head. The Order were a bunch of snakes, turning good men against each other. That was how they operated. Rotting organizations from within.

"How many people in the CIA know of Drake's treason?" he asked.

"Everyone at the top. We're trying to contain it but that's very difficult. He's vanished. We have a hit team trying to track him."

Jacob saw where this was going. Now was the perfect time to quit.

"Sir, with all due respect, if you want us to go find this asshole, I really—"

Tyler raised a silencing hand. "I'm not asking you to track him. We have another issue. Actually, two other issues."

"Sir, there's something I need to tell you."

"Once I'm finished." He turned to Jana. "I presume neither of you have heard from your father in the past week?"

"No," Jana answered, her voice growing worried.

Tyler shifted in his seat. "He has not been heard from since the earthquake. Eyewitnesses reported seeing a gunfight on the side of the mountain. Not the gunfight you were involved in, but further down the slope. The witnesses were at some distance but they could see one man was fighting against several and this man was eventually taken prisoner."

Jana took in a sharp breath.

"You think The Order kidnapped him?"

"They've been trying to kill them for some time now, as they have also tried to kill the two of you. I think for some reason they decided to capture him instead."

Jacob had a hard time imagining Aaron Peters surrendering. He must have been incapacitated.

Aaron …

That man had saved his life. No, saved his soul.

Jacob's mind had snapped while on duty in Afghanistan. He had gone feral. That was the only word to describe it. He had become more animal than human, killing everything in his path, including the American troops who had been sent after him.

Then the government sent Aaron Peters, who, instead of killing Jacob when he could have, captured him and nursed him back to sanity.

Jacob owed that man everything—his life, his mind, his relationship with Jana. Everything.

"We'll go after him, sir," he said.

His resignation would have to wait until after they saved him.

Tyler shook his head. "I'm afraid we can't at the moment, because we have no idea where they took him. Our intel in Turkey is a shambles after Drake fled and got our best local agent killed. We can't trust any of the other operatives in the nation either. The Order has no doubt used that chaos to get Aaron Peters out of the country to somewhere safer."

"But we can't just sit around and do nothing!" Jana cried. Her voice carried the sharp edge of panic, something Jacob hadn't heard since their very first mission. He reached over and took her hand.

"We won't do nothing, Agent Peters. While we can't go after the people who took your father, we can go after people from the same organization. The Order has reared its ugly head yet again."

"Where? How?" Jacob asked. *Damn, these people never stop!*

"In the past week, there have been attacks on three different disease research centers in the Middle East—at Amman, Basra, and Mosul. In all cases, they were hit in the middle of the night with overwhelming force and a variety of disease samples were taken. In all cases, the attackers called themselves the Syrian Front for Jihad and Martyrdom."

"I've heard of them," Jacob said, "but just barely. They're new and pretty small, aren't they?"

He tried to remember what he'd read in the regional reports. But he hadn't been paying as much attention to them as he used to. He'd lost interest.

Luckily, Tyler Wallace filled him in.

"The Syrian Front for Jihad and Martyrdom is a breakaway from al-Qaeda, just as ISIS was. Like ISIS, they are a Sunni organization sworn to kill all Shia. Unlike ISIS, they have not called for a caliphate."

"Smart," Jacob said.

ISIS had gained a huge amount of territory very quickly and then declared a caliphate, a nation ruled by Sharia law with the goal of expanding across the globe. That was a big mistake. Because by trying to be a nation with a capital and ever-expanding borders, they had lost the flexibility and hit-and-run tactics of a typical terrorist group. Now they had to defend territory instead of melt into the shadows. And by swearing to kill all Shia, they had made instant enemies of Iran to the east, the majority of the Iraqi population, and a large percentage of the population in Syria and Lebanon. That, as much as Coalition bombing, had led to their downfall.

"How strong are they?" Jana asked.

"Unclear. They only announced their formation a few months ago. Since then, they have conducted suicide attacks on various al-Qaeda, Kurdish, and Syrian government targets. This is a significant escalation. Firstly, they have never operated within Kurdistan. Hitting a research center in Kurdistan's capital Mosul was impressive, as was striking the capital of Jordan."

"So how does this tie into saving Aaron?" Jacob asked. Because if it didn't, he wasn't going to get involved. He wasn't going to crush yet another terrorist group only to see a new one form the following month. He was tired of playing whack-a-mole.

“We think The Order and Dr. Harlow are behind this. All three disease research centers are part of a World Health Organization program to categorize and study animal and human diseases. That’s their main objective. But they have a secondary program, also through the WHO, that studies ancient diseases. Archaeologists in the region analyze ancient bone and tissue samples and the researchers try and extract the DNA of extinct diseases.”

“I didn’t know diseases went extinct,” Jacob said, feeling more nervous. This might just be a bigger operation, like Wallace said. And if so …

"They can, or they can mutate," Jana replied. "Some ancient scourges like bubonic plague have mostly gone dormant, with only a few dozen cases globally per year. Luckily, that disease can be treated if caught early. Other diseases mutate into something milder, like what we're seeing with Covid now. Others die out completely. We have records for a number of diseases in the ancient records that no longer seem to exist. Bacteria and viruses are like other living species, they adapt and sometimes die out."

“And these idiots are trying to revive some ancient plague?” Jacob said. *Great. Just great.*

His boss nodded. “A plague for which we would no longer have immunity. While some new terror group wouldn’t have the technical means to replicate it, I wouldn’t put it past Dr. Harlow and The Order. I’m thinking The Syrian Front for Jihad and Martyrdom is more of a front organization for them rather than an actual splinter group. Aaron Peters has vanished without a trace, and the only way we can hope to track him is to target one of their operations.”

“But we don’t know it’s them,” Jacob objected. “Maybe these guys have a few university professors as members. It wouldn’t be the first time that happened.”

Jacob’s boss shook his head.

"In the attack on Mosul, the Kurdish forces managed to get to the scene just as the attackers were fleeing. They killed a couple of them and wounded one. As they closed in, trying to capture the wounded terrorist, he bit on a cyanide capsule."

Jacob groaned and looked at the ceiling. Avoiding capture by using a cyanide capsule was the trademark of The Order.

He had to go on this mission. There was no choice.

He was still stuck in the CIA.

We wondered if he would ever get out other than in a coffin.

CHAPTER THREE

The first duty of a prisoner of war was to escape.

Aaron Peters took this duty seriously. The challenge was how to put that duty into action.

He had no idea where he was or even what other rooms there were in this building, assuming it was a building and not a bunker.

All he knew was that he was in a five-foot by ten-foot concrete cell with nothing but a toilet and a foam pad and two thin blankets on the floor. There were no windows. The only exit was a heavy steel door with a hatch at the bottom, presumably to put food through.

He hadn't been given any food yet. He had just woken up a couple of minutes before, something that had no doubt been noted by whoever was behind the security camera in the upper corner of the room encased in a globe of bulletproof glass that he couldn't break.

He had already tried.

Now Aaron paced back and forth, limbering up muscles made sluggish from a long period of being drugged. He had been huffing up a mountain to the south of Trabzon, trying to get to where Jacob and Jana were fighting those cultists, when he got bushwhacked by a team of fighters from The Order. He ended up in a tight spot when who should appear but Roger Tyson, a CIA agent he'd worked with in Afghanistan a few times.

Roger had saved him and then promptly stuck him with a tranquilizer and boasted how he had joined The Order.

That crew was so crazy they would willingly let themselves get shot just so Roger could get in close and take him prisoner.

How did you fight an enemy like that? Sure, the Islamists liked to die for the cause too, but their religious fundamentalism made them predictable. There was no way to predict what The Order would do. He had been tracking them for years and had still not discovered their motivations.

How long had he been out? He was hungry and thirsty. Judging from the fact that he hadn't had any exercise while he was out, and that he was fully fed and hydrated when he got kidnapped, he figured that the level of hunger and thirst he felt equated to about twenty-four hours with no food or water.

He'd need some sustenance pretty soon.

The Order had already thought of that. The slit at the bottom of the door snapped open, and a tray shoved through. On it was a thick steak sandwich, an orange, and a large mug of water.

The slit snapped shut again.

"Want to talk?" he shouted.

No answer.

"Asshole," Aaron grumbled.

He took the tray. It was a flimsy plastic thing that wouldn't make a decent weapon. The food sat directly on the tray. No plate to break into shards to make a knife. The mug was thin plastic as well.

The Order had thought of everything. The Order always thought of everything.

Aaron sat cross-legged on the floor, flipped off the security camera, and began to eat. He didn't worry about the food being drugged. He needed to eat and drink. If he refused to, they'd find other ways to dope him up.

At least the food was good. They obviously wanted to keep him healthy.

For what? Most of the time, prisoners were fed just enough to keep them alive, but so little that they were left weak and unable to resist effectively.

Another mystery. Perhaps he'd find out more when whoever was behind that door came through to chat.

Aaron Peters didn't have to wait long.

The moment he put down his cup, having drained the last of the water, a hidden speaker came on.

"Put the tray on the far end of your cell opposite from the door. When the slit opens, put your hands through."

Aaron saw no reason to disobey, so he obeyed.

As soon as the slit opened and he put his hands through, someone clamped a pair of handcuffs on his wrists. He could feel the weight of a chain attached to them and hear it rattle on the concrete floor beyond his door.

"Now, put your feet up against the slit."

He pulled his hands back and saw he was trailing a chain attached to the links of the handcuffs. He sat down facing the door and put his feet against it. They had taken his boots, of course. And his belt.

The slit was too small to get his legs through, so the guy on the other end of the door had to stick his hands through to Aaron's side. Aaron resisted the urge to stomp on his fingers. That would be satisfying yet counterproductive. He didn't mind fighting a longshot battle, but he only picked fights he had a chance of winning.

The end of the chain was linked to a set of manacles that hobbled him so he couldn't go faster than an old man's shuffle. The chain attaching his wrists and ankles was too short for him, so when he got up, he could only stand at a stoop.

A common psychological tactic to make a prisoner feel vulnerable and submissive.

While Aaron Peters sure felt vulnerable, he had never in his life felt submissive.

"Turn your back to the door and take two steps forward."

Aaron did so.

The door opened. He heard heavy, booted footsteps behind him. Aaron scrunched up his face.

As he expected, hands reached around and put a blindfold over his eyes.

When he relaxed his face, the blindfold slipped down just enough that if he turned his eyes upwards as far as they could go, he got a thin slit of vision directly overhead.

Not much, but better than nothing.

Hands turned him around, and he got pushed into what he presumed was a corridor. He didn't have enough peripheral vision to tell.

He felt a cold muzzle press against his right temple, then another one against his left temple.

Yeah, yeah. You have guards ready to cap me if I try anything. Tell me a new one.

He shuffled along, guided by that pair of hands. No one spoke, and he didn't try to strike up a conversation. Instead, he watched the little he could see of the ceiling, just a thin strip half obscured by the fabric fluff at the edge of the blindfold, like seeing through the bottom of a closed door covered in gauze.

The ceiling had fluorescent lights and aluminum air ducts. That and the lack of ambient sound made him think he was in a bunker. The air smelled of machine oil. He heard the low hum of a generator. Aaron counted his steps.

After twenty-four steps, they stopped, and those hands spun him around several times. Obviously, they were at an intersection and they didn't want him to get his bearings.

Too bad for them. He could see a fire alarm directly above him. The little light that showed its battery was working pointed toward the corridor with his cell. He kept an eye on that. When they stopped turning him, they ended up facing to the right.

Then they walked straight forward sixty-eight steps and stopped again. Again, they went around and around. This time there was no marker on the ceiling around him and he didn't know which way he ended up facing.

A door opened in front of him. He was pushed inside. Not hard. They hadn't been overly aggressive. Perhaps they realized they couldn't intimidate him.

"Blindfold," someone ahead of him said. A male voice, mature and deep and accustomed to command.

They pulled off the blindfold, and he squinted. Two bright spotlights shone in his face, obscuring the features of three figures seating at a table between him and the lights. All he could see was that one was definitely a woman, and there was a stouter figure who was probably a man, and the third was a more fit man. He tried to turn to see the men who escorted him here. A pair of hands pushed his head back to face forward.

"Aaron Peters," the voice spoke again, coming from the fit male on the right. "The man who holds the world record for the longest time on a covert op. Kill count well over a thousand. Expert in martial arts, all known weapons systems, fluency in eight languages. I am sure you have many more skills of which we are unaware."

"I can break wind out of both ends at the same time."

"A Kipling reference. *The Man Who Would Be King*. Yes, you are well-read too."

"I think that line is only in the movie version and not the book. I can't remember. It was a long time ago."

"Are you tired, Mr. Peters?" the woman asked. *Not Agent Peters?*

"I've been sleeping for the past twenty-four hours."

"That's not what I meant, Mr. Peters. What I mean is, are you tired of fighting?"

"It would be nice if I didn't have to, but that's not the kind of world we live in. Assholes like you keep causing trouble."

The stout figure spoke. It was definitely a man's voice.

“We are trying to end trouble, Mr. Peters, not cause it.”

Aaron was pretty sure that he was hearing Dr. Harlow. Aaron had analyzed Dr. Harlow's declarations when he was blowing up hydroelectric dams, and it sure sounded like the same guy.

“Yeah, you folks really are trying to bring peace to the world.”

The woman replied. “Sarcasm is beneath you, Mr. Peters. While it may appear that we are the cause of strife, we are actually trying to end it.”

Here we go. Here comes the sermon.

Aaron was not disappointed.

“Imagine a world ruled by logic, by technocrats striving to eliminate pollution, eliminate poverty. Free humanity from all the evils and ills it has suffered since the last Ice Age.”

There was a pause, and the man who Aaron believed to be Dr. Harlow took up the slack.

“The ancient civilization we are trying to rebuild had freed mankind from all of that millennia before the pyramids were even dreamed of. This civilization lived a pure, clean lifestyle with a stable population and an energy source that did not threaten the planet.”

Then the mature man, the one who had commanded the guards, spoke. These three had obviously been rehearsing their pitch.

“I am sure you are privy to enough high-level macroanalysis of the global situation to know we only have another generation, two at the outside. Overpopulation, resource depletion, rising carbon emissions, increasing radicalization, migratory pressure, all of these factors will lead to a steady degradation of civilization. We are seeing the initial phases already, and it will only get worse. Mankind is wavering at the edge of a steep, slippery slope, and once we tip over, the slide into the abyss will get faster and faster until we cannot stop ourselves.”

“We intend to keep that from happening,” Dr. Harlow said.

“By blowing up a bunch of hydroelectric dams and killing tens of thousands of people?” Aaron asked.

“Regrettable but necessary. We kill tens of thousands to save millions. Billions. We needed to expose the Antiquities Division for what it was, a corrupt organization that was going too slowly to benefit mankind.”

Or benefit you. I’m thinking the Antiquities Division has the same endgame as you, but you want to speed up the process and ensure you end up on top.

“I presume I’m speaking to Dr. Harlow?”

Pause. "You are speaking to Dr. Harlow's representative."

Weak. You're not used to this stuff, are you? Research is more your line.

"Whatever. So you've gotten into bed with The Order. I presume at least one of you three is in that organization?"

"We are all members of The Order," the woman replied.

"And you share the same goals as Dr. Harlow here?"

"This is Dr. Harlow's representative," the woman said, avoiding the trap. "And yes, we do. The Order has long sought the very same goal—a unified world free of strife. We joined forces with Dr. Harlow's group when we realized he had the means to get us to the end we sought. You could be part of that end."

Aaron didn't say anything. He wanted to laugh, to make a snide comment, but he stopped himself.

He wanted to see where this was going.

The male leader type spoke next. "We don't expect to convince you ourselves. You have been trained to see us as the enemy." *Your actions trained me to see you as the enemy.* "So we will not appeal to your emotions but to your practicality. When you return to your cell, you will find a report on the state of the world. It is collated from the top sources of leading countries, institutes, and the international organizations such as the UN and the WHO. When you study it, you will see in just how dangerous a position this planet is in. The reports you have seen, that most of the public and even high officials have seen, are watered down in order to stop a panic and disruption of the global markets. This is the unexpurgated version. Read it. And then we will speak again."

The blindfold was put back on. Aaron didn't scrunch his face this time. The leader guy, and perhaps the woman too, would know that trick.

He was led back to his cell, locked inside, unshackled through the food slit, and discovered that his tray had been removed. In its place was a thick sheaf of loose paper at least five hundred pages thick. There was no binding, nothing hard that could be used as a weapon. Unlike so many enemies, now deceased, these folks were not going to underestimate him.

Aaron flipped through it. Lots of charts, graphs, and statistics. At the beginning was a table of contents that showed the document investigated every aspect of the world situation from the rise in global pandemics thanks to the increased ease of international transport to the projected limitations of fossil fuels. One large section described how renewable power such as solar and wind could only partially ameliorate the looming global energy crisis. Another section went into very technical detail about how nuclear fusion would never be a viable option. Then there were grim predictions about overpopulation and resource depletion.

The slit opened and another meal came in. Aaron's stomach grumbled, and he realized he had been flipping back and forth through the document for at least three or four hours.

It was absorbing stuff, assuming it was all true. At least some of it was true. He had no idea if all of it was. Some parts were too technical for him to tell. And it might all be skewed by a selective use of the evidence.

Aaron had no way of knowing. He ate his meal and considered his options.

He did know that his chances of escaping were slim to none.

That left him with only one option.

He studied the door. The hinges were set slightly out from the door and were of a style that had a small knob at the end. The upper one was a little over six feet from the floor. The bottom hinge, about two feet from the floor, had a knob pointing downwards.

His bed had two blankets atop a foam pad. He could the tie two blankets together and end up with about twelve feet of cloth. If he took the two blankets, wound them up really tight, and hooked one around the bottom knob, tie it off on itself, and then hook it around the top hinge, he might have a firm enough hold and enough slack to make a noose.

He'd have to work quickly, though. Or maybe ...

Aaron got up and studied the camera. It didn't look like it had infrared capabilities. Assuming they turned off the lights to allow him to sleep, which he thought they would since they were acting all buddy-buddy with the whole "good food and you should join our just cause" routine, then he could do it in the dark.

He took a deep breath and came to a decision. Tonight, he would hang himself.

CHAPTER FOUR

Amman, Jordan
The next day ...

Jana was trying really, really hard to keep it together.

Trying and failing.

She knew she had a job to do, and knew keeping her head clear was the only way she could have a hope of finding a clue about where they had taken her father. But keeping her head clear was proving impossible.

She had lost him for so long, and now, less than a year after reuniting with him, had lost him again.

To the worst enemies possible.

She and Jacob had just flown to Amman, posing as Interpol agents, their usual cover. While most nations would accept Interpol agents, no one wanted a visit from the CIA. She and Jacob had already made arrangements to meet with the head researcher at The Royal Center for the Control of Diseases. They would also meet with the lone surviving guard who was in an isolation ward at the central hospital. They needed to learn just what the terrorists took and any details the guard might have noticed.

The capital of Jordan was a sun-soaked city of mostly concrete buildings set on a series of hills. While older neighborhoods with wooden houses and some traditional mosques clustered here and there, the city had expanded greatly in the past few decades thanks to urbanization and successive waves of refugees from the wars in Iraq and Syria. Their taxi driver took a whole forty-five minutes cursing at traffic to get out to the eastern fringes of the city.

Once there, they could see the damage clearly.

The Royal Center for the Control of Diseases stood on a hill, isolated from any other buildings. Even as they approached from half a kilometer away, they could see a dump truck parked inside the gate it had rammed through. A police cordon was set well down the road, all the officers wearing surgical masks.

"God preserve us," the taxi driver muttered in Arabic. There had been no way to keep the news secret, and everyone in Amman was probably worried about it.

The driver certainly was. He left them a good two hundred meters away from the police cordon.

“My daughter is pregnant with her third baby,” was the only justification he gave.

“Blessings on your daughter and her family,” Jana replied in Arabic.

“Thank you,” the taxi driver replied.

That did not make him drive any further. Jana didn’t blame him.

They got out and approached the police cordon, where they were met by a police captain and a woman in a lab coat and headscarf. Both Jordanians wore surgical masks. The woman handed them a pair.

"I am Rana Bisarat, the chief scientist here at the research center," she said in careful but correct English. "We are thankful for Interpol's help. I have been in contact with my colleagues in Mosul and Basra, and we have come to some conclusions about what the terrorists might have been after. First, let me show you the lab and the damage there."

“Pleased to meet you, Dr. Bisarat,” Jana said. “Let’s get to work.”

They both put on their masks and walked up the slope toward the research center. The sun was strong and their faces began to sweat behind the masks.

And here I thought I was done wearing these things, Jana thought.

They got to the gate and saw several chalk outlines of bodies just beyond. Beyond those stood the research center. The doorway was sealed with a plastic sheet with a zipper on it to make a door.

“There is little risk of infection at this point,” Dr. Bisarat said. “We removed all disease samples and sprayed with disinfectant. But still, we require hazmat suits.”

She indicated a rack near the door with suits of various sizes hanging from them. Jana and Jacob found ones that fit and put them on. The researcher and the police captain did the same. The suits were even more stifling than the masks. Jana hoped they had the air conditioning on in there.

The researcher unzipped the entryway, and they clambered through in their awkward suits. She zipped it back up and then unzipped an identical barrier a few feet beyond.

They found themselves in a hallway lined with offices. Looking through a couple of open doors, Jana saw that the computers were missing. She also saw a trail of blood drops leading to a door at the end of the hall.

“That’s from Private Jamal Obeidat,” Dr. Bisarat said. “The sole survivor. He was shot through the hand and forced to guide the terrorists through the building.”

“How is he doing?” Jacob asked.

"He doesn't seem to have contracted anything, but they're still doing tests at the hospital. As for his wound, he lost a lot of blood but will recover."

Jacob glanced at Jana. He still wore a high-collared shirt to hide the bandage over his neck wound, just like Jana still wore a hat to cover up her bald spot from her head injury.

We’re in no shape for this, Jana thought. *Not that we have much choice. We have to find Dad.*

A spike of panic pierced her heart. She suppressed it. Emotion would only get in the way of the mission.

They passed down the hall and came to a large laboratory. All the computers were missing. To one side was a walk-in freezer, its door hanging open and the many steel shelves lining the walls wide open. The freezer unit had several bullet holes in it. A chair sat right in front of the doorway. A large puddle of mixed refrigerant fluid and condensation covered the floor of the freezer and part of the lab.

Dr. Bisarat clicked her tongue and gestured at the scene. “As you can see, they tied the poor private to this chair and left him right in front of the melting samples. It’s doubtful he caught anything, though. The police responded quickly and released him, then sealed off the area. The initial response unit is also in isolation. None of them are showing any symptoms. Besides, the terrorists took all the most virulent diseases.”

“What did they take?” Jana asked.

“SARS, AIDS, Yellow Fever, Avian Flu, and … some others that don’t make any sense.”

“What were those?”

“Well, in addition to studying modern disease, this center and the others in the network study ancient diseases. We work with archaeologists who get samples from ancient bones and tissue in order to study the development of diseases in the past. We had twenty-eight such samples here. The terrorists took them all. It's strange because they couldn't make any sort of bioweapon out of them. They're just ancient DNA, not living cultures like the SARS."

Maybe some terrorist splinter cell couldn't make them, Jana thought, *but Dr. Harlow and The Order sure could.*

"We'd like a list of all the diseases taken, ancient and modern."

"Certainly. This was a coordinated attack against our colleagues in Kurdistan and Iraq. I'm not sure why they hit three diseases centers. We all have more or less the same living cultures."

That's because they weren't after the living cultures. They stole those just to put us off track.

"So what was on these computers?" Jacob asked.

"All our research. We have backups, of course, but the terrorists stole all the research for all our projects, both the collective work we have done and the individual research by each scientist. It's a terrible breach of data. Frightening too. They want us to fear they'll make a bioweapon. That's why they tied poor Private Obeidat to that chair. To stoke fear."

"I think it's time we met him," Jacob said, looking around. "Unless there's more you wanted to show us here."

"We can go to the hospital. The police are studying the security footage. We'll show it to you before we go. There's not much to see. All of the group wore masks and gloves. The van they drove away in was found burned fifty miles out of town in the desert."

"Let's go," Jana said.

***

Private Jamal Obeidat lay in an isolation ward, his hand bandaged. The bedside table was crammed with get-well cards, a box of dates, and another of sweets. A soccer match was on the television. He watched it listlessly, obviously suffering from mental shock and depression.

The soldier looked like a kid, one of the millions of young recruits in their late teens who throughout the Middle East had to do a year or two of national service to boost army numbers and train the citizenry in case of a general mobilization.

He turned to look at them as they entered in their hazmat suits.

"More needles? You're making me look like my grandmother's pincushion."

"No needles this time, Private Obeidat," Dr. Bisarat said. "I have two American agents from Interpol here with me and they have a few questions for you."

"Oh, all right. Do they speak Arabic? My school back in Safawi had the worst English teacher in all of Jordan. We used to check YouTube and correct him."

Jana grinned and said in Arabic, "My colleague and I have worked in the Middle East for many years, Private Obeidat. We're both fluent in your beautiful language. While I'm sure you gave a full report to the police, could you tell us what you saw? Anything unusual?"

"Well, I guess you've reviewed the security footage."

Jana and Jacob nodded. They had both watched the attack unfold on the recordings. The young soldier went on.

"So you saw how they did it. What the cameras didn't show is what they said."

"Such as?"

"They acted very strange. They wanted me to point out where the laboratory was even though there was a big sign. It was like they wanted to pretend to be illiterate. But when they got to the lab, they pulled out lists of the samples they wanted and read the labels. And they kept saying the name of their group. They obviously wanted me to remember. I'd never even heard of this group. I don't pay attention to that stuff. The jihadists are all crazy."

"Did they make any political statements?" Jana asked. The police captain had already told her that they had not, but it was good practice to repeat questions with witnesses in case they had left a detail out or just remembered something.

Private Obeidat shook his head. "Just the usual stuff about our country being in bed with the West. Why? Because we let women show their faces and don't cut the heads of Christians? Stupid. Oh, one strange thing. They put the samples in their pockets like they didn't care about keeping them frozen. You'd think they would bring a cooler or something. Or maybe they wanted to be martyred. They mentioned that. Maybe they spread across the city and are carrying diseases in their pockets all over the place!"

The young soldier's eyes grew wide at the idea.

"That wouldn't work very well," Dr. Bisarat told him. "The samples are very small and might not infect anyone."

"Oh." He looked reassured. Then his eyes went wide again. "Wait. They're going to reproduce them and make a bioweapon!"

Smart kid, Jana thought. "That's something we're looking into. It would help if you didn't spread that idea around. We don't want people to panic."

"Maybe they should panic! There could be all sorts of diseases going around! We need to evacuate the city!"

The police captain gave Dr. Bisarat a look that said this guy was getting another couple of weeks of isolation.

Poor kid. He's just a small sample of the kind of reaction we're going to get if this splinter cell manages to deploy a bioweapon for real.

Jana did not think the terrorists were simply walking around with open test tubes in their pockets. They kept one man alive for a reason—to be a witness. They wanted him to think that's what they'd do, because a low-ranking kid like him would know little or nothing about the ancient disease research program and would never dream that such biohazards could be replicated.

They could, although it would take an advanced lab and a team of specialists.

"Take care, Private Obeidat. The doctors tell me you didn't catch anything. They just need to keep you for observation."

The young man nodded. "That's what they told me too."

He did not sound convinced.

From the hospital, the police drove them to their hotel in central Amman and left with the promise that they'd send over all relevant documents. By this time, Jana and Jacob were tired and hungry, so they went to the hotel restaurant, a rooftop terrace that gave a sweeping view of downtown. They ordered some shish kebab, which came with a generous plate of bread and a big bowl of olives, and tucked in.

"I'm starving," Jana said. "Once we're done here, we need to look at those documents the police are sending us."

Jacob looked at his phone. "Yeah, I just got a ping that they've arrived. Judging from the file size, we have some reading to do."

"You do the modern stuff. I'll look at the archaeology."

"Fair enough."

Jacob looked out over the rooftops. A couple of minarets stood in the distance. The lines on his face had grown deeper, and his eyes lacked their usual sparkle.

"You feeling better?" Jana asked.

"Yeah, my neck's fine."

"No, I mean in general. You were liking that R and R we had before the last mission."

"I liked the R and R we had on the mission before that too."

"Neither were long enough." She paused, then asked the question that had been on her mind for some time. "Are you burning out?"

Jacob shifted in his seat. "I can't afford to burn out."

"Yeah, but you've been going full on ever since you came to my dig in Morocco and that was almost two years ago. You must be exhausted."

"I can't afford to be exhausted."

Jana looked down at the table, picking at the edge of her napkin. "I know. You're as close to my dad as I am. It's just that … I get the feeling that you're not as into this work as you used to be."

Jacob shrugged and looked out at the skyline. "It's not really up to me. I … " His voice trailed off and he focused on something in the middle distance.

Jana turned to see what it was. Before she could pick out anything strange, he dove for her and threw her to the floor.

Taken unawares, she wasn't able to cushion her fall and smacked her head against the tiles.

Consciousness snapped out like a light being switched off.

CHAPTER FIVE

Jacob cursed as a potted plant sitting on the edge of the wall exploded just next to where he had been sitting.

A glint of sunlight off a bit of glass had warned him a sniper was positioned on a rooftop a few streets away. The crack of the rifle shot came to them faintly over the buzz of traffic and the conversation of the other diners.

All those conversations stopped, replaced with a confused babble about what just happened.

"Shooter!" Jacob shouted. "Everyone down!"

He repeated the command in Arabic and French in case some people didn't get it. A few people were quick to hit the deck. All Arabs. They were sadly accustomed to this, even in a relatively peaceful city like Amman. They took threats seriously. They began to pull down the slower diners.

Jacob peeked over the edge and saw the gunman still in place three streets away. He ducked back down moments before a bullet cracked off the concrete inches from his head.

"Jana, we need to … "

Jana was lying on the floor, out cold.

Oh God, she hit her head when I took her down.

Another shot rang out. A tourist who hadn't gotten down cried out and grabbed his shoulder.

Damn. The shooter thought that guy was me.

"Everyone stay on the floor!"

Jacob had wasted his words. After the guy got hit, everyone else got the message and hugged the floor so closely they looked like they wanted to melt into it.

The rim of the roof had a waist-high barrier of concrete. It looked bulletproof. If everyone stayed down, they'd be safe enough.

But what about Jana? She needed to get to a hospital to have her head injury rechecked. She'd gotten a serious concussion less than two weeks ago.

That would have to wait until the active shooter was neutralized.

Giving Jana's hand a squeeze, Jacob got up and peeked over the lip of the wall at a different location than before.

The sniper took another potshot at him, the bullet buzzing close overhead.

This guy doesn't miss a beat.

Jacob ducked down again. He had seen what he needed to see.

Running low to keep beneath the top of the wall, he got to the stairs. A waiter cowered nearby.

He grabbed the waiter's arm. "Call the police and call an ambulance. My wife is injured."

Wife? Jacob thought as he got to the stairs and rushed down them three at a time. They always posed as husband and wife when travelling in the Middle East. Some hotels didn't let you stay together otherwise. But this time he didn't need to pose, not with this hotel and certainly not with some waiter pissing his pants. It had just come out.

Focus. You got an active shooter on a roof three blocks away and you have to neutralize him.

Something he had done dozens of times before, except this time he didn't have any weapons.

They had gone straight from the airport to the crime scene and hadn't had time to meet with the local CIA fixer to arm themselves.

That was going to be a problem.

Jacob made it down to the ground floor and darted out the front door of the hotel. As soon as he did, he ducked low to the right. Just as he expected, the sniper took a shot at him. The building the guy had chosen was situated perfectly so that he could cover both the rooftop and the front entrance.

The bullet clonged off one of the four brass stars set into the wall under the hotel's name. The star fell to the sidewalk with a clatter.

"Worse than a negative Google review!" Jacob quipped, then realized he didn't have an audience.

No one appreciates my humor. Even Jana would have rolled her eyes at that one.

Jana ...

God, I hope she's OK.

Jacob lost sight of the shooter's building behind another structure as he ran down the street. He zigzagged as he crossed an exposed intersection, traffic blaring angrily at him, and got back under cover of another building.

No shot had come. Was the sniper trying to make an escape? He had probably heard Jacob's reputation and didn't want to die with Jacob's hands around his neck.

Jacob kept sprinting up the street, people turning to stare. A cop in front of a government building shouted something after him. Jacob didn't check to see if he was giving chase. A couple of cops as backup would be a good thing.

One block. Two. The building stood another block away and across the street. Jacob slowed and began to move with care.

By now, the sniper must have realized Jacob was coming for him and was either staying put, hoping for another shot, or getting the hell out of there.

Jacob hadn't gotten a good look at him. Slim man. Blue baseball cap. Tan shirt with long sleeves.

If he was at all smart, he'd do a quick change before heading out.

Jacob rounded the corner and saw the building. A row of parked cars gave him some cover. No one looked over the rooftop. Jacob kept an eye on it.

The building was an apartment building with shops on the ground floor. The entrance was further along the street Jacob was walking on. The door was open, and a pair of women stood in front of it, chatting.

Just then, a man came out. Slim. No cap. Gray, short-sleeved dress shirt. Carrying a guitar case.

The guitar case clinched it for Jacob. He picked up some speed. The guy didn't even look his direction as he casually walked the other way.

Oh, you're an icy one.

Jacob had to do this just right. He had no doubt the guy had a pistol or something in those loose trouser pockets, or maybe he'd just pop open that guitar case and plug him with the rifle. It probably had a folding stock to fit in the case, but at short range it would still shoot just fine, stock or no stock.

The guy thought he was getting away and playing it cool. That gave Jacob the first move.

But what move? He was almost to the building entrance now. If he didn't go in, the sniper would know Jacob was onto him and things would get very nasty very quickly.

Then, a moped puttering up the street gave him an idea. Just as it passed by a large van parked by the side of the road, blocking the view of the sniper, Jacob stepped in front of it.

The rider skidded to a stop. He was in his late teens and stared in bafflement at this crazy foreigner stepping out into the road as if on purpose.

The poor kid reminded Jacob of Private Obeidat.

In one fluid movement, Jacob flipped him off the bike and landed him on his feet. The boy let out a squawk. Jacob caught the moped before it fell, hopped on, and did a 180 before its stunned owner had time to react.

Jacob sped off, or at least sped off as fast as its underpowered engine could make it go.

He had to swerve left to avoid a car, then swerve right to avoid another one. Only when the drivers shouted curses against his lineage did he realize he was driving the wrong way on a one-way street.

The sniper turned around, whether from the sound of the cursing or the sound of Jacob's stolen moped, which must have made the sniper think a swarm of mosquitos was descending on him.

He looked right at Jacob, and there was no surprise or confusion on that face.

That proved to Jacob that he had found his man. He bumped over the curb and hit the gas, hoping to run him down.

The guy reached for the clamps on the guitar case, realized he wouldn't get it open in time, and swung it at Jacob's head.

Jacob ducked, and the moped rammed right into the guy.

That impact flipped the bike, launching Jacob into the air. He tucked into a roll, wished his still-healing neck wound good luck, and hoped for the best.

The best did not happen. He had hoped to land in a practiced roll and end up back on his feet, ready to kick some ass. Instead, he slammed right into a telephone pole. Jacob let out a grunt and flopped unheroically on the pavement.

The world had a rough time stabilizing itself. For some reason it got all topsyturvy and blurry.

Jacob managed to sit up. He clutched his neck. No blood. Good. Finally, the world got stabilized and clear.

The sniper was just picking himself off the ground, pushing away a couple of older men who had come to help him up. A woman with a shopping bag in each hand shouted at Jacob in English, "You crazy tourist! Do you drive in your own country like that?"

"Sometimes. If I really need to."

The sniper grabbed the guitar case and opened it.

Uh-oh.

"Gun!" he shouted.

To their credit, all three passersby moved out of the way.

Giving the sniper a perfect shot at point-blank range as he pulled out the rifle from the guitar case and aimed without even securing the folding stock.

Why bother at this range?

Jacob tucked into another roll and launched himself at the sniper's feet. A bullet chewed up the pavement just behind him, and then Jacob made a second impact in less than a minute.

At least the sniper's legs were softer than that telephone pole.

Easier to knock down too. The guy fell flat on his face.

He didn't drop his gun, though. A pro.

Jacob spun around and kicked him in the stomach. The man grunted and tried to raise his rifle. Jacob grabbed the barrel and wrenched it upwards. A shot rang out, the bullet flying straight in the air to make a long parabola and land … somewhere.

Jacob hoped it didn't hurt an innocent person. At the moment, though, he was more concerned he didn't get shot himself. The guy kicked out at him and tried to wrench the rifle free.

He landed a foot right on Jacob's elbow, sending a spike of pain up his arm, followed by numbness.

"Ow! Why do they call it the funny bone?"

That made him let go with one hand. The sniper pulled with all his might and broke free, so Jacob threw himself on him, batting the gun aside and digging his hands into the man's throat.

Unable to fire his gun, he smacked the butt against Jacob's head. Jacob held on, pressing harder on his throat.

Another bash to the head, not as hard this time. The man was weakening.

Then he broke. Instinct took over, he dropped the gun, and he tried to pry the fingers away that were clenching shut his windpipe. They struggled for a moment, but Jacob was on top, straddling his body and pressing down on his legs to keep him from moving.

I'll ease up once he's barely conscious. Can't risk killing him. I want to—

The click of a cocked revolver made him look up.

And he found himself looking at the muzzle of a pistol about five inches from his eye.

CHAPTER SIX

Jana woke up with a splitting headache and little spots of light dazzling her vision. She found herself lying on a sofa. She didn't remember Jacob laying her down on a sofa. That would have been far more romantic than throwing her down on the tile floor in front of a bunch of other diners.

There must have been a threat. She looked around to see if there still was.

She found herself on a sofa on the hallway of the hotel, one of those common yet little-used pieces of furniture that hotels put in various spots just so the hallway or bathroom doesn't look too empty. This was the first time she had ever actually used one.

Next to her stood a very-concerned looking hotel manager, one of the waiters, and two Jordanian police officers.

"Hi. Um, ow!" When she tried to sit up, pain shot through her skull like an ice pick and she saw more stars. She sat there a moment, gripping the edge of the sofa, taking deep breaths. One of the police officers was saying something, but she didn't catch it.

"Sorry. I hit my head. What was that?"

"What did you say?" the cop replied.

Oh, I forgot to reply in Arabic. She switched to that language.

"Sorry. I hit my head. I'm a bit confused. What did you say?"

"We have detained your husband, the other Interpol agent."

"Huh? He's not my husband. He's with the CIA."

Jana rubbed her head, thinking that might not have been the right answer. She still felt confused.

The two police looked at each other.

"You will need to come with us."

"She's been hurt!" the waiter said. "We need to have her checked out first."

"Silence! This is police business!" the officer snapped.

"I'm trying to help you, sir," the waiter said, suddenly submissive. "What if her condition gets worse? What if she's someone important?"

The policeman looked back toward the rooftop terrace. "The emergency personnel can look at her once they treat that victim's bullet wound."

A moment later, a pair of men dressed in white carried one of the other diners by on a stretcher. The police summoned over a third man who looked like a doctor.

"Examine her. She has a strange wound and is acting confused."

The doctor came over and gently touched around the shaved portion of Jana's head. It was only then that she realized she no longer wore her hat.

"What is this wound?"

Jana's mind was clearing a bit now. She realized she had let slip way too much information. How could she have done that? Damn, that fall really jiggled her brain. She still had a piercing headache too.

"What is this wound?" the doctor asked again.

Oh, right. Gotta answer.

Jana picked her words carefully.

"I fell and hit my head against the edge of a steel table."

"This looks like the graze from a bullet."

"Um … "

"They say you hit your head when your husband threw you to the floor to avoid the sniper."

"How is he?"

The policeman answered that. "We found him fighting with a man carrying a rifle. Both are in police custody until we clear up this matter. Why would someone be trying to kill you?"

"We're here investigating the attack on the disease center. Call the captain in charge there. He'll back us up."

"Does he know your husband is in the CIA?"

"What?"

"Are you in the CIA?"

The doctor cut in. "She's in a fragile condition. Let me do my examination. Did you hit your head?"

"Yes."

"Are you feeling pain? Blurry vision?"

"The vision has cleared up, but I still have one hell of a headache."

The doctor shone a penlight in her eye, then in the other one. The little light felt like a miniature sun. In fact, even the ambient lighting was too damn bright.

"Do you have a ringing in your ears?"

"No."

She had at first, but that was gone now.

"Do you feel nauseous?"

"No. Can I see my partner now?"

"I think we need to take you to the hospital for more tests."

"Is Jacob all right?"

"He didn't get injured," the police officer said. "But we've detained him for questioning. You two are not acting like Interpol. You can't detain suspects in this country."

"He was a sniper who almost took us out."

"Don't worry, your husband isn't under arrest, but he does have a few questions to answer."

Looks like I'm going to as well, Jana thought. *I need to keep my head clear.*

The medics returned with the stretcher, and the doctor gently had her lie down.

"I'm fine," she insisted. *I need to find Dad.*

"You are not fine, miss. Let us take you to the hospital."

No, I am not fine. But I don't have time to be hurt.

***

Two hours later, at the hospital, the doctor finally let her go. Her splitting headache had eased to a dull ache, and all the other symptoms had disappeared.

For the moment. Jana didn't trust her head anymore.

"You need complete bed rest for at least two days," he told her. "Stay in your hotel."

"I will."

Yeah, right.

Jana was beginning to understand Jacob's loss of enthusiasm. Keeping this up for years must have been exhausting for him.

She left the examination ward to find Jacob waiting for her. He had a new bandage over his neck wound.

"Did you get hurt?" Jana asked, hurrying to him. She slowed when she felt a bit unsteady on her feet.

They embraced. Jana used the opportunity to lean on him. That felt better in more ways than one.

"It started oozing blood. I shouldn't have headbutted someone in my condition."

“They said they detained you.”

“Third World bureaucracy. Dr. Bisarat from the disease center got me out of it. She has connections as well as smarts.”

“A woman needs both if she wants to get anywhere in a Middle Eastern nation, even a moderate one like Jordan.”

Jacob took both her shoulders in his hands and studied her. “How are you? Sorry I knocked your head.”

She grinned. "You knocked me out. It hurt like hell, but it's better than getting plugged by a sniper."

“You sure you’re OK?”

"Yeah, yeah." She looked around at the other members of the public, anxiously waiting for their loved ones getting treated beyond the double white doors. She lowered her voice. “You got the sniper, right?”

Jacob replied in a whisper. “He’s being questioned by the military. They stepped in pretty quick and took him from the police. Oh, and somehow they found out I was CIA.”

Jana flushed. “Sorry. I slipped. A cop was grilling me just as I was regaining consciousness.”

“Yeah, the military and the police are making a stink with the embassy. We’re still free to move around, though. Tyler Wallace made a few calls. They know they need us.”

“Do you think we can be present at the interrogation?”

“Not sure. I have the number of a certain Colonel Munif. Let’s see if we can come over to play.”

***

It turned out Tyler Wallace had already talked to some general, who in turn called Colonel Munif, and the colonel welcomed them with open arms.

The colonel met them outside the main gate of a Jordanian army base at the edge of the capital. He was a short man with broad shoulders, thick arms and salt-and-pepper hair and moustache.

"Welcome, my friends!" he said in English. "Sorry, those sonofabitch bureaucrats got their panties on fire because you are CIA. I love the CIA. They helped us killed many of Saddam Hussein's soldiers. I was in the march on Baghdad when I was younger. I wish I got to strangle that little Iraqi turd."

“Your English is quite … expressive,” Jana said.

"I learn from U.S. Marines, biggest bad asses in the world except for Jordanian Special Forces. Those are the real ass-kickers. God *damn*, you should have seen what we did to an ISIS incursion last year. For *real*!"

Jana and Jacob traded a look. Colonel Munif ushered them inside.

"Would you like a tea? Maybe something stronger? I am a Muslim, so I don't drink any crap, but I always keep some crap for special guests."

"Thank you, but we'd like to see the suspect," Jacob said.

"Suspect? Ha!" The colonel slapped him hard on the back. "This isn't Judge Judy. The man is guilty as hell. As guilty as Osama Bin Laden, may dogs piss on his grave."

"He was buried at sea," Jana said.

Colonel Munif gave her a broad wink. "Suuure. The Navy SEALs kill him with one shot and bury him in secret. Don't kid a kidder. You brought him to Guantánamo and tortured him until his black heart gave out. I bet you put him in front of a mirror and chopped off his fingers and toes one by one, a new one each day."

"Is that what you're doing with the sniper?" Jacob asked.

Colonel Munif smiled. "Oh, we have more subtle ways. Don't worry, my friends. Soon we will find out who sent this sonofabitch."

Jana sure hoped so. The sun was setting, and the samples from the lab could be anywhere by now.

She shuddered to think what was being done with them.

Time was ticking, and the only lead they had was a sniper who had every reason not to talk.

CHAPTER SEVEN

The desert of northeastern Syria
That same evening ...

"The last of the samples has arrived, general."

General Tariq al-Rashid looked up from his desk in his Spartan office at his second-in-command, Qa'dan al-Nimir.

Qa'dan al-Nimir was a lean, wiry man of Bedouin stock with a hawk nose and glittering eyes. His hands were covered in the traditional tattoos of his tribe, marks with a meaning that only the Bedouin knew. During the Gulf War, a stray Coalition bomb had hit the tents he and his extended family lived in, killing almost all of them. Qa'dan al-Nimir had been only a baby then and didn't remember the incident, but he maintained a burning hatred in his heart.

That hatred made him very useful.

"Did they arrive in good condition?" Al-Rashid asked.

"Yes, sir. The laboratory says they have everything they need."

"How long until they can begin replication?"

"They are already working on it, sir. But you know how these scientists are. Soft."

General Tariq al-Rashid chuckled and put a handon his shoulder. "They are city dwellers and soft in the physical sense, my friend, but they are warriors of a different sort."

Qa'dan al-Nimir snorted. "Playing with their little test tubes and tapping away on their computers?"

"Come, my friend. Let's take a walk. I have been stuck inside for too long today, and while I am not Bedu, I long for the wide-open sky and the clean air of the desert."

They left the general's office, where he had been working on the dull necessities of running one of Syria's biggest factions. Supply. Recruitment. Negotiations with gun runners. People thought that a warlord did nothing but lead his men into battle. If only. No. Most of the time, he was stuck behind a desk or around a conference table like some Western businessman or Gulf oil sheik.

The office was in a converted common room of a private house he had confiscated in the isolated village of Al Atlal, near the eastern end of his territory. His army controlled a large swath of desert in northeastern Syria. While this territory included only a few decent-sized towns, little agriculture, and only a few mines and oil wells, it did have a border with Iraq, providing plenty of opportunities for trade, legal and otherwise. This was the source of the wealth for the Syrian People's Front.

That and an extremely generous donation from an oil sheik in Dubai.

They stepped outside and into the last light of evening. To the west, the sun was setting in a golden haze of a beauty only seen in the desert. General al-Rashid spotted a rare smile on Qa'dan al-Nimir's lips. A true Bedouin. He loved the subtle beauty of what so many others saw as only wasteland.

They walked down the main street, a dusty lane lined with a few shops, most of which were already closing. A few of his men strolled along or were posted at corners. They saluted him as they passed. The local women ducked into alleys or doorways. The local men kept their eyes averted.

Good. Fear was a useful tool of governance. So was loyalty, and many in his territory saw him as a strong leader who didn't impose a harsh interpretation of Sharia law like ISIS, who his faction had helped destroy. There were no crucifixions in the town square, no public lashings for listening to the radio. He also made sure his men kept their hands off the women. General al-Rashid had also built up the economy as much as he could in this war-ravaged and divided land.

It only took a couple of minutes to get to the end of the street, cross a small plaza, pass through a collection of scattered houses, before they were in the open desert.

Al Atlal wasn't much of a village, barely five hundred people when he had taken it from ISIS. He had made half those people leave so he could take the center of the village, where all the houses abutted one another, clustering together for protection as desert villages did, and cut holes in the walls to make a large, interconnected fortress of barracks, armories, and workshops. The rest of the villagers he kept around so it looked normal from spy satellites. You never knew when the Americans Russians or Israelis might be watching. Each group constantly sold Intel to rival factions in the endless deadly chess game of the Syrian Civil War.

As the two warriors passed through town, they attracted a small following of young boys. They wore faded old t-shirts handed down from older brothers or cousins, patched jeans or shorts. Those who didn't go barefoot wore cheap plastic sandals. There was nothing to do in these little towns except dull schooling and football on the dusty stretch of desert that passed for a pitch. Al-Rashid had promised himself that he'd build the local boys a proper soccer pitch, but there had been no time or resources. There was never enough time or resources for everything.

That would change soon. Very soon.

Most of the boys kept their distance, admiring the two hard men but not having the courage to approach them. No girls followed them. Girls stayed home where they belonged.

A couple of the braver boys, about twelve years old, plucked up the courage to walk beside them. Their friends laughed nervously. The two boys glanced back at them, basking in their approval, or perhaps seeking support.

"Where are you going?" one asked.

"You're Asif, aren't you?" Al-Rashid asked. "The best footballer in Al Atlal."

"No, that's me!" a smaller boy shouted from near the back. The boys burst into laughter.

"I'm the best," Asif said, puffing out what passed for his chest.

Al-Rashid smiled.

"I'll have to watch one of your games and decide for myself. And as to your question, we're going to the ruins."

"Are the tanks going to pass through again?" asked Asif's friend. The general recalled that his name was Muhammed.

"That was a sight, eh?" the general said, tousling their hair. "Did you enjoy riding on them?"

All the boys' eyes went wide and they burst into a cacophony of excited accounts of riding the armored column through town. Al-Rashid smiled. Good public relations. These boys would be the next generation of fighters. He would need a lot of them. He had many lands to conquer.

"I heard they smashed Al-Nusra," Asif said, eyes bright.

"They certainly did," the general confirmed. "Broke right through their line and made them retreat fifty miles."

It was a good victory over one of the most radical Islamist factions. What the general didn't tell the boys was that they had lost three tanks, and two more had broken down. He had also lost seventy fighters and gained no useful resources.

Just another pointless battle in this endless civil war. Al-Nusra's counterattack was equally pointless. They gained back twenty miles and both sides lost more men.

The factions in Syria were too evenly matched for any one of them to win, and they all hated each other too much to band together. The big powers—America, Russia, Israel, Turkey—all wanted to make sure Syria stayed divided and weak. The same with Iraq. They feared what the Arabs used to be and didn't want them to unite and rule once more.

And they would get what they wanted as long as the equation didn't change.

Those shipments from the disease center would change the equation, because thanks to that donor from Dubai he had been able to build a state-of-the-art lab. His officers begged him to spend that money on weapons. Tanks and rockets. Even attack helicopters. The donation had been that big. Al-Rashid had replied that the lab would give them better weapons than tanks or rockets.

It would give them weapons his enemies couldn't defend against.

The general and his second-in-command walked across an open stretch of desert toward a low mound, followed by a small crowd of diminutive admirers. The sun had almost set now, and the desert would soon grow cool.

"The call to prayer will come soon," Al-Rashid said. "Remember to pray, boys. We are not insane like ISIS and al-Nusra, but we are still Muslim. That's what makes us strong."

"That and the tanks!" Asif chirped.

Al-Rashid laughed.

"Tanks aren't the only type of weapon. Faith and strength are the most powerful weapons of all. Do you know my name?"

"Of course. You're General Al-Rashid. The greatest general in Syria!"

Not yet, boy. But I will be.

"That's not my real name. I took on the name to hide my identity from President Assad's secret police, who were hunting for me because I tried to assassinate him. I took my name from a great Muslim from the past. Do you know who Harun al-Rashid was?"

"Sure," Asif said. "A great Muslim from the past. Right?"

The general suppressed a groan. What passed for education in rural Syria was a joke. Half of these children couldn't read. Even worse, they didn't even know their own heritage.

The corruption of the Jews and their Western puppets reached even into the little schoolhouse of Al Atlal. Their history books had "Printed in Cairo" on them, but everyone knew who the government of Egypt took their orders from.

"He was one of the greatest caliphs of the Abbasid Caliphate," the general explained. "This was the early high point of Arab power, when we were expanding and spreading Islam as fast and as strong as a sandstorm across the world. 'Al-Rashid,' as you know, means 'Right-Guided.' He was right-guided by Allah, and that is why he had so many victories."

"Did he have tanks like the ones we saw?" one of the smaller boys asked.

"This was long before tanks. He had swift horses and swords." He put a hand on Qa'dan al-Nimir's shoulder. "And he had brave Bedouin tribesmen who scouted far ahead of his columns and made lightning attacks on the camps and rearguard of the unbelievers. Ah, here we are."

They had come to the ruins, the place Al-Rashid liked to take his walk to every evening. The boys had learned his routine and often followed him here.

Al-Rashid knew it was dangerous for him to have any sort of routine. A sniper or a drone might target him. So many leaders had died that way. But he couldn't help it. This place gave him a sense of peace, and a sense of purpose.

The weathered old mound rose five meters above the surrounding sand. At its base, one could discern weathered rows of mudbrick. Further up the mound, the ruins became clearer. Some stone blocks still stood one upon the other, and near the top were the fallen remains of some Corinthian columns.

"Do you know what this is?" Al-Rashid asked.

"The ruins," Asif said. "You come here at sunset to plan strategy."

I come here to get some peace and perspective, my young friend.

"Do you know the significance of this place?"

Al-Nimir looked bored. The Bedouin considered themselves a practical people, and if ancient ruins didn't mark the location of a well, then they were of no interest.

Asif thought a moment. "You said that it's a bunch of old towns built on top of each other and that the earliest was from when everyone was an unbeliever."

"Very good! You are intelligent, and we need intelligent people in my army."

Asif beamed with pride. They walked up the mound.

"We play up here sometimes," one of his little friends said. "My cousin found an old coin here a few years ago and his father sold it in the city for a fifty thousand pounds!"

"Was this before the war?"

"Yes."

"Good."

That would have been a fair amount of money then, enough for the man to buy himself and his whole family a new set of clothes. Now the Syrian pound traded at 13,000 to the U.S. dollar. No one wanted Syrian pounds. In all his international transactions, General al-Rashid used dollars or euros or something solid like gold. How humiliating. The man trying to reunify his country couldn't even buy a single bullet with his own national currency.

He and his second-in-command slogged up to the top of the mound and Al-Rashid sat on the capital of a Corinthian column. The boys gathered in a half circle like a unit, waiting for instructions from their commander before going on a raid.

"This mound is at least two thousand years old. This bit I'm sitting on is from the Islamic village that once stood here almost a thousand years ago. They reused this capital from a Roman site that is buried beneath our feet. While this region was part of the Roman Empire, Syrian soldiers made up some of the best troops in that great empire's legions. They were stationed as far away as Hadrian's Wall. That was a great fortress the Romans built in the north of England to keep the Scots out of the Empire. Beneath those levels are older towns, and older ones still, back some two thousand years or more. We Syrians have a long history, my young friends. The European nations can only count a few hundred years. Germany and Italy only became nations in the nineteenth century. America only became a nation in the eighteenth century. We are older, and have lasted longer, because we are stronger."

His gaze strayed to the north, where another, smaller village stood a kilometer away. That one held his laboratory. The key to his upcoming victory. He had been very careful to hide it. No one from Al Atlal was allowed there and from the air it looked like nothing more than a simple, almost deserted village, like so many in a region where much of the population had fled to the safety of larger towns. He had a few of his men act like they were doing regular tasks like herding goats, and even had some dress as women, much to the amusement of their colleagues, to do the washing and draw water from the well.

The people of Al Atlal must have known something was going on there, but they had no idea that he had built one of the most advanced biowarfare labs in the Middle East.

That had taken a long time and many resources. Some of his officers still maintained that they should have spent the money on more tanks and drones. They were short-sighted. His knowledge of history had taught him that the most powerful weapons came from the past.

"So when do we reunite Syria?" Asif said, plopping down next to him on the old column capital.

"Soon, my young friend. Soon."

"Can I help?"

General al-Rashid chuckled and put an arm around his narrow shoulders.

"Oh, Syria will be reunited long before you grow into manhood. But don't worry, my little warrior, the world is big. By the time you're grown, we will be conquering Italy. Perhaps by then we will even be sailing across the ocean to conquer America."

Asif gave him an uncertain smile, and the other boys traded looks.

Their hero worship was struggling with their sense of reality.

I know it sounds fantastical, my little warriors, but you will see. Oh yes, soon everyone will see.

***

Aaron Peters had waited until nightfall, just as he had planned. He had eaten the dinner they had given him and then had lain down when they switched his light off. He had lain there for an hour, ears perked for any sound in the corridor. Other than once hearing footsteps, muffled and indistinct because of the thick steel door, he had heard nothing.

Now it was time to act. While the camera didn't have infrared, a small amount of light peeked through the crack beneath the door and around the feeding slit. It was barely enough for even his dark-adapted eyes to see anything by, but someone watching on the other end of that camera might notice movement.

He had to do this subtly, and yet the final act had to be done quickly. He had to hang himself before they could stop him.

Aaron had already moved the lower blanket to his side, covered by the upper one. Now, with his back to the camera and his body hopefully shielding his movements, he slowly wound it up like a rope. Then he eased the upper blanket off and did the same, doing so with gradual, steady movements that would not likely catch the eye in such near darkness.

Once he had the two blankets coiled into semblances of ropes, he tied one end to the other and ended up with ten or twelve feet of rope. One end he tied into a tight knot so it wouldn't unravel. The other end he tied into a noose.

Doing this in the dark only by feel was tricky, but he took his time. Through his long career he had learned the value of patience, even to the point of being patient making the rope he would hang himself with.

It was the only way to get away from these people.

Now that he had his hangman's rope, Aaron had to move quickly. They would probably notice if he got up. Maybe not that very instant, but soon. And then he wouldn't have much time. Maybe two minutes at the outside.

He hesitated, steeling his courage.

Time to do this … *now.*

Aaron Peters crept as quickly and smoothly as a panther over to the steel door.

He hooked the knotted end of the rope around the bottom knob hinge, tied it off on itself, and then played out the rope and hooked it around the top hinge. He yanked them hard, getting them tight, then looped the noose around his neck.

Was that running footsteps he heard in the distance?

Too late, fellas.

He pulled his head forward, and the noose went tight around his neck. Then he tucked his legs up so his full weight was pressing down on his neck.

Aaron's head throbbed as the air cut off from his lungs and brain.

CHAPTER EIGHT

The cell door flew open, making Aaron swing along with it. His head banged against the steel, and the noose tightened even more around his neck. Dimly, he was aware of his legs drumming against the door, making it ring like a snare drum. His heart felt like it would tear from his chest. His head felt like it would explode.

Then a strong set of arms grabbed him around the middle and lifted him up. Still, the air was gone from him, the noose maintaining its grasp like a boa constrictor.

The light came on, but Aaron could not see clearly as great patches of black obscured his vision.

He heard voices, but they were indistinct, distant.

Then he slumped forward, muscles loosening, arms going slack, eyes closing.

"Hurry up!" someone shouted.

Cold steel against his neck. A tug. The noose came free.

It took all of Aaron's willpower not to breathe in a great lungful of air to relieve the terrible burning inside him. Instead, he took in a slow, steady inhalation through his nostrils. He kept his body loose.

"He's not breathing!"

"Well, resuscitate him! We need him."

"Mouth to mouth?"

"What else? Hey! Call the medic!"

"Ugh."

Aaron felt himself being stretched out on his back on the cold concrete floor. Someone touched his face.

Just then, Aaron gave his lungs what they so desperately wanted by sucking in as much air as they could hold. He brought his hand up, palm first, opening his eyes.

His vision was still blotted with black spots but his instincts remained true and his palm strike hit the man bending over him.

Aaron had meant to strike at the nose and break it, but he felt more than saw his hand hit him on the chin.

Good enough. The guard's head whipped back.

Aaron pushed him off and tried to rise.

His vision grew dark, and he stumbled to his knees. Again he took a greedy breath, his mind and vision slow to clear. He took another.

That was the last he got to take. The second guard, who had been calling out to someone in the hallway, turned around and saw his friend lying stunned on the ground and the supposedly suicidal prisoner trying to get up.

He lunged for him with a Bowie knife, no doubt the same knife he had cut the rope with.

Aaron was just able to block the blow at the last moment, turn, and drive the thrusting arm into the concrete wall. The knife glanced against the hard surface and dropped from the guard's grasp. Aaron then swung around to get him in an arm lock.

He was still too weak. The guard tore free and clocked him a good one across the face. Aaron staggered back, lungs still working, his system desperately trying to replace the oxygen Aaron himself had cut off.

When the guard came for him again, Aaron ducked to the right and tried to trip him, but the feint was clumsy, slow, and the man darted back before Aaron could strike.

The man drew back even more and reached for his pistol.

Aaron risked it all on a flying kick. The man tried to dodge and almost made it, the foot aiming to cave in his stomach only hitting him in the hip, spinning him around and putting him off balance. When he landed, Aaron made a spinning punch that hit the guy right in the temple, more by accident than anything else.

Good enough. He fell to the floor with a thud, unconscious.

Gasping, Aaron scooped up the pistol just as the first man rose. He shot him in the gut and ran out of the cell. His head had finally cleared, even though he still felt weak. He kept his lungs working hard.

He found himself in a corridor lined with several cells. The corridor dead-ended about twenty meters to his right. To his left there was an intersection, and beyond that another one. The second one looked the right distance to be the one where they had spun him around.

Rounding the closer intersection came a man dressed as a medic and a burly guy with an assault rifle. Their eyes registered shock. The man with the gun tried to raise it.

Two shots took them out.

Aaron ran over to them, glanced down each side of the intersection and saw nothing, then grabbed the assault rifle and the guy's spare clip.

Aaron was excruciatingly aware of the security cameras mounted at regular intervals along the corridor. His every movement was being monitored, and every fighter in this complex would be gathering to take him out.

He didn't have much time.

Where was he?

There wasn't much clue. He was certainly underground in an extensive network of tunnels. That told him little. The few labels he saw on ducts and the cameras were simply corporate logos or in English. Once again, that told him little. The people he had seen belonged to various ethnicities and the guards had spoken English as a common language. There had been accents, but he had been too out of it to identify them.

Not that it mattered. The Order was an international organization.

So, he had no idea where he was or how big this complex was. He only knew his cell and how to get back to the interrogation room.

Not having anywhere better to go, he went there.

Down to the second intersection where the familiar fire alarm shone its beacon light. A look to the right showed a dead-end passage with two doors opposite each other. Damn. When they had spun him around, he had lost his bearings. He had no idea which door was the right one.

That choice was put off for a moment as a man peeked around the corner of the intersection behind him. If Aaron hadn't been constantly looking over his shoulder, he would have been shot for sure.

As it was, Aaron ducked around the corner just in time for the bullet to whine past him.

He crouched low, peeked around the corner, and didn't see the guy. That guard was smart enough to know how quick Aaron was, or had been warned.

Never mind, he'd peek around the corner sooner or later.

Before that happened, a door between them opened up.

Aaron put a bullet into whoever it was coming out.

He must have only winged him because the door slammed shut.

That just left him and the guard.

And whatever hordes The Order had closing in on him.

He didn't have time for this.

The guard knew that too, and took his sweet time exposing himself.

Aaron counted to five, and when the guy didn't show, fired again down the corridor. He wasn't firing at anyone, but hopefully the guard would think that he was and that he was staying in position.

Nothing could be further from the truth. Instead, he sprang up and rushed to the two opposing doors, one of which was the interrogation room.

He had no real reason to go here except it was the only spot familiar to him, that and the vague hope that Dr. Harlow or one of the other commanders might still be in there.

Aaron got to the two opposing doors and had no idea which one was the correct one. He tried one, found it unlocked, and swung it open just in time to step inside before three shots cracked off the doorframe in rapid succession.

Aaron glanced in the room just long enough to see that it was unoccupied, then peeked around the door and returned fire.

The guard had already ducked behind the corner.

Aaron gave another glance and saw that he faced a storeroom with several steel shelves holding cardboard boxes labeled with numbers.

When the guard peeked around the corner again, Aaron was ready for him. His shot winged him and the guard cried out, clutching his face and ducking back out of sight.

That would keep him quiet for a while, but backup was coming sooner rather than later. Aaron rushed across the hallway and tried the other door.

He found it unlocked. When he opened it, gun at the ready, he found he was back in the interrogation chamber.

It was unoccupied. All he saw was the long table and three chairs where Dr. Harlow and the two others had sat, and the pair of floodlights, currently unlit, standing behind.

At one of the spaces sat a closed laptop.

A shout made Aaron peek out in the corridor. It was the guy he had hit, calling for help.

A trick? They might already be gathering out of sight around that corner. The Order was trained in obfuscation.

He looked around, unsure what to do. All he knew was that he couldn't stay here. This was a dead end, and the enemy was gathering. He pulled out the half-used magazine from his assault rifle and snapped a fresh one in. Nothing to do except make a charge down the open corridor.

Almost as suicidal as that attention-getting fake suicide he had done in his cell.

But something made him pause. Not fear—Aaron Peters had lived way beyond fear—but curiosity.

That laptop.

He gave the corner a final look and, not seeing any sign of imminent threat, rushed over to the laptop.

Hoping it wasn't encrypted, he opened it.

There was no screen, no keyboard, only a thin steel container inside and a nozzle pointing right at him.

A nozzle that shot out a cloud of odorless gas.

Aaron choked and emptied his lungs, waving his hands in front of his face as he rushed around the table and away from the trap.

He barely got to the other side of the table before the room began to rock, and his gait became unsteady.

"Damn it," he muttered, hearing the slurring of his words.

He got to the doorway, almost stumbled outside, and corrected himself, only to bang against the wall next to the doorjamb.

Aaron stood there a moment, breathing in what he hoped was pure air, his head spinning.

Then, in slow motion, his knees buckled and he slid down the wall to the floor.

He heard voices. Footsteps. The sounds came distorted and distant. Aaron tried to raise his weapon and it slipped from his grasp. His vision blurred. He felt like he was floating.

It took him a minute to realize he was being carried.

His head began to clear a little, although his movement remains sluggish, uncoordinated. They laid him down somewhere, probably his cell, and before that heavy door slammed shut, he heard the voice of Roger Tyson, the CIA agent who betrayed him, whisper in his ear,

"Rest easy, buddy, and tomorrow we'll get to work. It won't be long until you see things our way. I guarantee it. You don't think you can turn, but you can. Trust me, buddy, you can."

CHAPTER NINE

Jacob stood in the interrogation chamber with Jana and Colonel Munif. The sniper was strapped to a metal chair bolted to the floor. He had been stripped down to his underwear, doused with cold water, and sported a few bruises Jacob didn't remember giving him.

The interrogation chamber was in a concrete cellar. Even fully clothed, Jacob found it chilly. Several soldiers lounged around, including one guy who looked like his mother had put steroids in his felafel. He had raw scrapes on all his knuckles and an evil look on his face.

"I'd start talking if I were you," Jacob told the prisoner. "Personally, I don't believe in torture, but these guys don't give a damn what I think."

The prisoner didn't reply. Jacob turned to Colonel Munif.

"I presume you've put him through the database?"

The U.S. and all its allies shared a large database of known members of terrorist organizations. Some profiles had detailed bios complete with photos and even fingerprints. Others had little more than an alias and an affiliation to a particular group.

"We ran his face through the scanning software and didn't come up with anything," one of the soldiers said.

"Did you do that before or after you hit him so hard that his face swelled up like a watermelon?"

Nobody answered, which was all the answer Jacob needed.

He sighed, then asked, "Has he said anything?"

"Some details about your mother."

"I mean anything important."

A soldier grinned. "He said—"

"I don't care what he said. You're not going to get me angry enough to torture him. People lie under torture. It's a terrible way to get good intel."

The big man with the scraped knuckles looked at him like he was an idiot. Jacob ignored him and turned to the prisoner.

"Look, buddy, you know the drill. Your life is basically over unless you come clean and tell us everything we want to know."

The man spat at him. Jacob was expecting this and dodged a glob of bloody phlegm. Jana, standing behind him, had to dodge too. The gunk splatted on the floor to add another spot to the constellation of stains.

The brute with the scraped knuckles hit him in the back of the head. The prisoner grunted and flew forward. He would have gone down if the chair hadn't been bolted to the floor.

"Stop that!" Jacob shouted. Not that he wanted to play Good Cop to the room full of Bad Cops, but someone that big punching a man in the back of the head can cause a hemorrhage that can lead to death.

Jacob grabbed a strip of cloth lying on a table that was probably meant to be used as a blindfold, dipped it in a bucket of water sitting ready to be splashed on the victim, soaked it, and went over to wipe the man's face. Then he wrapped the cool cloth around where the brute had punched him. The prisoner was too dazed to spit at Jacob again.

"You are too soft on this piece of crappy," Colonel Munif said. "We should pull his finger out like the CIA did with Osama Bin Laden."

"That's not going to make him talk," Jacob grumbled.

He crouched down in front of him and looked at the prisoner's hands. Ink stains on the fingertips.

"They took your fingerprints. I bet they're checking them now. Are you in the police database?"

The man looked away.

"So you are," Jacob went on. "That's bad news for you. When they find out who you are, they'll bring in your family. You want them to end up in a room like this? You want your sisters to end up in a room like this?"

The man grimaced. Jacob wasn't just doing this to get him to talk. He wanted to keep it from happening. These guys were thugs in uniform. While he had a hard time feeling sorry for this sniper, his family didn't deserve to be mistreated.

One of the guards started to say something, but Jacob raised a silencing hand and the man stopped. He had become accustomed to walking into a room and dominating it. Being a secret agent from an allied superpower helped. His fluency in Arabic helped more. The fact that these bullies could see he could floor any three of them helped the most.

The sniper didn't meet his eye.

"Come on," Jacob continued. "It's only a matter of time before they find out who you are, and then they'll round up your parents, your brothers and sisters, cousins, whoever they can get their hands on. All those innocent people, all those people you grew up with, are going to end up in a place like this. I don't want that. And I'm sure you don't want that."

The sniper shuddered, let out a big sigh, and seemed to deflate.

"General Tariq al-Rashid," he said so fast that it almost came out as one word. It was like he was forcing the truth from his own mouth.

Jacob glanced at Colonel Munif, who looked as confused as Jacob felt.

"General al-Rashid?" Jacob asked. "Of the Syrian People's Front?"

"Yes," the sniper said, his head hanging low.

"You're not with the Syrian Front for Jihad and Martyrdom?"

"It doesn't exist. We just made it up as camouflage."

"Why?"

"The general didn't want to lab attacks traced back to us."

"Terrorists always brag about their hits. Why the change in strategy?"

The sniper looked up for the first time, pride and defiance in his bloodshot eyes. "Because we aren't a terrorist group. We are an army of national liberation."

Colonel Munif snorted. "Not terrorists? The Syrian People's Front set off a dozen car bombs in Damascus and other Syrian cities last month."

"We are going to overthrow the Assad regime and put true Arabs in control, Arabs who will restore our culture to greatness."

"By blowing up car bombs," another soldier said. "I swear to Allah, you are the dumbest man I know."

"We target Assad's oppressive forces."

"By blowing up car bombs outside police stations where innocent passersby get killed too," Colonel Munif said, landing a vicious right hook on the prisoner.

"That's not helping," Jacob said, getting between the sniper and the officer.

"It's helping me feel better," Colonel Munif replied.

Jacob ignored him and turned back to the prisoner. "So why hit three disease research centers? You making a bioweapon?"

"I don't know the details of those operations. My post is here in Jordan."

Colonel Munif cocked his head. "Wait a minute. You have a Jordanian accent. At first, I thought you were faking but it hasn't changed at all through the interrogation."

The prisoner nodded. "I am Jordanian."

"Then why work for a Syrian militia?" Jacob asked.

Again that defiant gleam. "Because it is so much more than that. We are going to bring back the greatness of the old Caliphate."

"I've heard that one before," a guard said. "Al-Baghdadi is dead and so are most of his followers. Raqqa is a pile of rubble."

The prisoner clicked his tongue.

"Not a caliphate like ISIS. They were radicals. Crazy people. They killed more Muslims than the Americans. No. We are making a true caliphate like at the beginning of Islam, when the righteous swords of faith were conquering every land. We'll do that again. General Tariq al-Rashid will lead us to a glorious future."

"You're not going anywhere," the big man with the scraped knuckles growled.

The sniper gave him a haughty look. "Al-Rashid's army will roll through Amman soon enough."

Jacob looked at Jana.

"Looks like we got some work to do."

He had a feeling they had gotten all they would get out of this guy. The Jordanians would continue to work on him, of course, but Jacob didn't want to be around for that.

He had saved the man's family by convincing him to talk. There was nothing he could do to save the prisoner.

God, I'm sick of this crap.

Jacob and Jana left the interrogation room while the soldiers closed in on their prey.

CHAPTER TEN

Three hours later back at a different hotel room, this time guarded by a pair of Jordanian secret police, Jacob and Jana had found some answers.

They had trawled through all the data they could find on the Syrian People's Front and its leader General Tariq al-Rashid.

There was a lot more information on the militia than there was on its leader.

The Syrian People's Front came out of the chaos of the Syrian Civil War, which started in 2011 and had been continuing its relentlessly bloody drama ever since.

The civil war had started small, as these things often did, but that small start was the spark that set off the inferno.

The crops had been bad. Many farmers in Syria's hinterland, already trying to scrape a living from a harsh land, were pushed to the edge. They had been promised support from the President Assad's dictatorial government but that aid hadn't arrived.

So the farmers did something no one ever did in Syria—they staged a protest in the capital.

This was unheard of. It didn't matter that it was peaceful. It didn't matter that the protestors had legitimate grievances. Any show of defiance was considered treason.

So Assad's troops opened fire.

It's unclear how many died. Many more were arrested, and the survivors fled to the countryside to lick their wounds.

Assad probably thought it was over. It was not.

Because seeing innocent farmers getting gunned down in the streets was the last straw for a society that was thoroughly sick of secret police, an unfree press, economic stagnation, and no opportunities.

Suddenly there were more demonstrations, mirroring the protests of the Arab Spring all over the Middle East. These were met with more brutal reprisals. But the demonstrators wouldn't be stopped. A weakness of military dictatorships was that every male had to serve in the armed forces, which meant they all knew how to fight and the reservists all had firearms at home.

Soon, the demonstrators were firing back.

The situation went into freefall pretty quickly. Factions formed. The Islamists started getting weapons from Iran and Sunni radical groups. A democratic coalition seeking to build a new Syria on the Western model got clandestine support from the U.S. and Europe. The Kurds, Christians, and other minorities formed their own militias. The only thing all these groups had in common was they wanted to oust President Assad.

But President Assad did not fall. He still had a large base of support in the army, whose officer corps knew they wouldn't survive a successful revolution, and they got a large amount of money and munitions from Russia. While Assad lost about half the country, he kept the capital and managed to firm up the front lines. The rest of the country fragmented into various factions, weakened further by the rise of ISIS, who slaughtered the factions as much or even more than it went after Assad's forces.

But ISIS turned everybody against them, from the smallest Christian militia fighting for its very survival to the U.S. Air Force, which bombed the living crap out of them. Their Caliphate crumbled, and much of the land they had taken in Syria went to a relatively new faction.

The Syrian People's Front under its leader General Tariq al-Rashid.

The faction formed out of the decline of Islamic State. While ISIS retreated out of its territory in Syria, various factions that had fought it began fighting each other again. Many of the rank and file were sick of this sort of thing, and a relatively small local militia in central Syria, one of the many self-defense leagues in this lawless region, began to grow, calling in fighters under the banner of national unity, the fight against radicalism, and a deep-seated hatred of the Assad regime.

This was very attractive to what passed for moderates in the civil war. Even some of the Syrian Democratic Forces moved over to the banner of the Syrian People's Front, fighters who had never been democratic diehards and who were attracted by General al-Rashid's strong leadership.

The group grew. It gained credibility by not fighting against any faction other than Assad and the Islamists, assuming no one attacked them first. In the areas it controlled, it ruled with an iron but fair hand. Dissidents weren't tolerated, of course, but the Syrian People's Front did away with strict Sharia law. If you kept your nose clean, their security forces left you alone and you could enjoy a modicum of economic stability.

Basically, General al-Rashid was acting like a less-bloodthirsty version of the Assad regime. For a nation weary of war, that was good enough for a lot of people.

But who was General Tariq al-Rashid? The CIA dossier wasn't clear on that. The name was clearly an alias. He himself admitted that, saying he took it on because he aspired to unify all Muslims and create an empire like the Caliphs of old. A laughable goal, and the CIA report stated it was doubtful many of his men fell for it.

Jacob wasn't so sure about this assessment. The sniper certainly seemed sold on the idea.

As to the general's identity, there were several theories. One was that he used to be an officer in Assad's army who got sick of the old regime and left. This had become common in the second phase of the civil war when things got bloody. Initially, everyone in the military toed the line, but as the bodies piled up and cities got destroyed one by one, some of the more intelligent officers saw this as a pointless waste and either fled the country or joined one of the resistance groups. General al-Rashid's tactical acumen and leadership ability certainly hinted at a former military post.

Now his forces controlled much of northeastern Syria, holding their own against the regime's army and the Islamist Al-Nusra, and signing a truce with the Kurds and the Syrian Democratic Forces. Most recently, they had had a fairly successful offensive against Al-Nusra.

At the moment, they weren't much on the CIA's radar. They weren't being supplied by any major side. The U.S. preferred arming the Kurds and the Syrian Democratic Forces, the Iranians supported various Shia groups, and the Russians threw their weight behind Assad. Instead, the Syrian People's Front used their position on the Iraqi border to make money from both legitimate and illegal trade.

That had worked well for them, as had the economic stability they had fostered. Through taxes and import fees they had decent funding and were able to buy plenty of weapons on the international arms market. With these and a good supply of manpower, they were able to hold about a fifth of Syria. Even so, their borders hadn't changed much in the past few months. They were able to hold their own but not expand. Perhaps with these raids on the disease centers, General Al-Rashid was looking for a game-changer.

While Jacob had been delving into the background of the group, Jana had been looking at some of its current activity. This is where they struck gold. She had found a report from the French secret service that an agent believed to be working for General Al-Rashid had arranged the purchase of a large amount of lab equipment. Supposedly this was hospital equipment to rebuild the area's shattered healthcare system. The Syrian People's Front was making a big deal about this in their propaganda. In reality, intel hinted that this lab equipment could be used to make diseases rather than cure them.

That had been the suspicion of the French agent's report three months before the attacks on the disease centers. Now, that assessment appeared to be correct.

The order had come a month after a large donation from a bank account in Dubai. The French had looked into it, and after peeling away the layers of several shell corporations, found nothing beneath. Whoever had coughed up two hundred million dollars had covered their tracks well. The French had no idea where the money had originated.

The French report noted that the equipment went through Beirut, a common nexus for all sorts of illegal merchandise, and that a certain import/export dealer who made money smuggling on the side was responsible for the transfer of the equipment from its European suppliers across the border into Syria. The French agent wasn't sure how the equipment made it across the territories of two different factions to make it safely to General al-Rashid's territory, but in a war zone anything is possible with money.

Jana had a suggestion.

"Since this smuggler handled such a sensitive operation on his own, I'm thinking he's more than just a supplier for the Syrian People's Front. I'm thinking he's a supporter."

Jacob nodded. "You might be right. Perhaps we should pay him a visit. It might give us a better idea of what we're facing."

"We could use the help of this French agent. His name has been redacted."

"I'll call up Tyler Wallace and find out who he is. The French can be a pain, but when the chips are down, they can be relied on."

"Let's call him now. I'd like to ask him how the search is going for Dad."

Jacob put an arm around her. Until she had said it, he hadn't noticed just how strung out she looked. The strain must have really been wearing on her.

"How are you holding up?" he asked in a soft voice.

She gave a little shrug. "I just wish we could help more. I feel useless pursuing this other mission."

He kissed her on the forehead. "You heard Wallace. This could be connected. It's got the fingerprints of our enemies all over it. That anonymous donation is just the kind of thing Dr. Harlow and The Order do."

Jana sighed. "I know. I just wish we could go after him guns blazing."

He gave her shoulder a reassuring squeeze. "Knowing how our missions turn out, it will probably come to that soon enough."

They called Wallace on their secure satellite phone. He picked up.

"Agents Snow and Peters. I heard about the sniper incident. Everything all right over there?"

"Yes, sir," they responded.

Jacob gave a brief rundown of what they had learned and asked for the French agent's name in the report.

"I'll send that right over to you. Yes, I think that Beirut connection is worth following up."

"What's happening with the search for my father?" Jana asked.

"We are working on a number of leads."

Jacob squirmed with impatience. That didn't sound promising.

"Are they finding any good intel?"

"Nothing solid, but they're still searching."

I hope the lead we're following is solid. It feels pretty damn thin.

"So we're nowhere closer to finding out where they took him?"

"The search teams are still working, Agent Peters. I understand your impatience, but you need to let our people do their job. He was kidnapped by experts who have evaded capture for years now. It's not going to be easy to track them down. I'll keep you updated as soon as we know more."

Jana grimaced and shifted in her seat. Jacob reached over and squeezed her hand.

"In the meantime, I'll get to work on getting you as much intel on the Beirut smuggler as I can," Tyler Wallace said. "I think you should get the next flight to Beirut."

Jacob nodded. That seemed like the best plan. There were only two problems with it.

One, if this smuggler was the local agent for the Syrian People's Front, he would have plenty of backup.

Two, the last time he had been in Beirut a little over a year ago, his cover had been blown. He had been avoiding the city ever since.

CHAPTER ELEVEN

Beirut, Lebanon
The next evening ...

Jana was about at the end of her patience. After a restless night plagued by a lingering headache, she and Jacob flew to Beirut. While the sniper hadn't revealed any more information, Tyler Wallace had been good to his word and reached out to the French.

And hit a bureaucratic brick wall.

The Directorate-General for External Security, France's equivalent of the CIA, didn't want the give authorization for releasing their local agent's name and they wouldn't reveal the reasons why. Wallace had insisted, stressing the time-sensitive nature of the situation. The French said that although they understood his predicament, they had security issues of their own to deal with and they needed more information about the situation, requiring the CIA agents to come to Beirut and get in touch.

This left Wallace with a problem, as he updated them in several phone calls. He couldn't be sure his contact in the DGES wasn't working for The Order. After it turned out the CIA's Ankara bureau chief was part of that organization, Wallace had become even less trusting than before.

So they ended up in a situation where the DGES needed more information about why they should divulge sensitive information, and Jana's and Jacob's boss at the CIA couldn't tell them anything. Wallace eventually got around this by calling in a favor with someone in the French government, who called someone who called someone, and eventually Wallace got the name of the agent.

"Hervé Boucher," Wallace told them. "He poses as a businessman to the Lebanese government and as a smuggler to the Lebanese underworld. I'm sending over his contact information."

It's about time, Jana thought. It was already evening of the following day, and her headache hadn't improved. She didn't tell Jacob about it. They had too much to do, and she didn't want him to get distracted.

Jacob called Boucher, the French agent having already been alerted that he would, and the DGES agent offered to meet them.

They found him at a café overlooking Beirut's western beach. Here there were plenty of beachside cafes and restaurants catering to the few foreigners who did business here and the few locals whose finances had survived Lebanon's economic slump to go out in the evenings. A warm breeze blew of the Mediterranean and Lebanese families strolled along the beachside promenade.

Many of them carried flashlights. Much of the city was unlit, thanks to a chronic power shortage. Many of the cafes and other businesses had their own generators, which hummed in the background, ruining what could have been a tranquil night. The country was broke, and that opened the door to all sorts of crime.

Hervé Boucher was a small, trim man who looked every inch the prosperous businessman. He sat at a table, legs crossed, a cigarette dangling from between long fingers. He wore a fine French suit and looked more at home at a board meeting than investigating smugglers and terrorists.

At least at first glance. Jana's dad had trained her to look beyond the obvious, and she noted how Boucher had his back to a large pillar, that his movements showed a pantherish grace, and that his eyes never stopped looking all around him.

He spotted them instantly, signaled with his eyes, and then kept on looking at his surroundings.

Someone sent him our photos, Jana realized. *I wonder if the DGES has a dossier on us?*

Probably, considering how we helped with the Louvre robbery case.

Boucher crushed out his cigarette, rose, and shook their hands with a firm grip.

"Pleased to meet you," he said in cultured French that spoke of an expensive education, "Do sit."

Jana found it interesting that he assumed correctly that they spoke French, but perhaps that was in the dossier too. She wondered just how much the various national intelligence agencies knew about her, and whether they knew more, or less, about Jacob.

They sat. Boucher had picked a table a little apart from the others. Even so, they kept their voices low.

“My superiors inform me you are investigating that medical supply shipment that went to General Al-Rashid.”

Jana nodded. “We think it’s linked with the robberies of three different disease control centers in the Middle East in the past few weeks.”

Boucher took a drag from his cigarette and blew the smoke out of his nostrils. “I warned them this might happen, but as usual those in control like to talk more than they like to listen.”

“So true,” Jacob replied. “What can you tell us about this smuggler?”

“Salim ibn Omar. A wealthy man in the import/export business, and like so many of his kind, the bulk of his income comes from importing and exporting illegal merchandise. He exports Lebanese hashish to Europe, and imports weapons from Russia and Serbia.”

“But the hospital lab supplies were above board?”

“At least on paper. From what I can tell, they included many dual-use laboratory items, plus some things not on the list. I don’t know exactly what, but I’m thinking equipment for creating bacterial cultures and similar equipment.”

“Is this Salim ibn Omar a follower of the general?”

“Publicly he is neutral. But as with many Lebanese, he had family in Syria, so he has a stake in the civil war. While I haven’t found definitive proof, my instincts tell me he follows General al-Rashid. He’s made several shipments to him and I can’t find any evidence he’s shipped to any of the other factions, when he could make a great deal of money doing so.”

“Interesting. Have you made contact?”

“Yes, I’ve worked with him many times.”

Jana raised an eyebrow. “Worked with him?”

“Such a man can prove useful for our purposes as well as those of other powers.”

Jana paused, and when no other information seemed forthcoming, she said,

“So what does he know you as?”

“An arms merchant.”

“I … see. Any chance we could meet him?”

Boucher sighed and lit another cigarette from the stub end of his last one.

“You are going to ruin a perfectly good contact, aren’t you?”

“Why do you say that?”

Boucher chuckled and waved his cigarette in an expansive motion, encircling them with its smoke.

"Because your reputation precedes you. I did not know your name before this day, Agent Snow, but I knew that you leave chaos in your wake."

"Gee. Thanks."

The Frenchman chuckled. "I anticipated your request and already sent a message to Ibn Omar requesting a meeting. We can meet him tomorrow. I will say that you two are colleagues of mine who are getting more involved with the Lebanese part of my operation. We will then arrange some arms shipments, or at least pretend to. This will give you a chance to feel out Ibn Omar and decide how to proceed from there."

"How well guarded is he?"

"Very. And we will be searched before meeting him. I would suggest a higher level of guile than your reputation grants you."

***

The meeting didn't happen until noon the next day. Jana had slept better, and the pain in her head had ebbed to a dull ache. While she felt more energetic and focused, it worried her that she still had a headache at all.

What worried her more was that there was no update from Tyler Wallace about the search for her father.

I should have never left Turkey. I should have tried to pick up the trail there.

Too late for that now. They were heading for a warehouse at the edge of town. Boucher was driving a Mercedes with tinted windows while Jacob rode shotgun and Jana fidgeted impatiently in the back.

All three wore business suits, and they were all packing 9mm pistols concealed in shoulder holsters. That didn't make her feel any better since Boucher had warned them they'd have to give them up before they got to see Salim Ibn Omar.

Jana looked out over the city. She had been here a year and a half ago with Jacob on their very first mission together, when he had been a near stranger and not a welcome one. Her father had spent more time training him than seeing his own daughter, although now she understood the reasons why. On that first mission, Jacob had needed her knowledge for a mission and against her better judgement, she had gone along with him.

They had ended up here in Beirut and nearly lost their lives. The first time among so many.

And since then, they had been on almost a dozen missions together. She had reunited with her father and forgiven him, and had fallen in love with the man she had once resented.

So much had changed, and yet so little.

The world was still under threat. The world was always under threat. It's what kept men like Jacob Snow and Aaron Peters busy, running from flashpoint to flashpoint, trying to stop everything from falling apart.

And now it was keeping her busy, too.

She closed her eyes and touched each finger of her right hand to her thumb, one after another from her forefinger to her pinky. Then she reversed the order. After that, she did the same with her left hand. It had been a test the doctor had performed on her in Amman and she had failed at first. The following day, she still did it a bit clumsily. Now, she did it perfectly.

Good. But why did her head still ache?

She didn't need to be going on a mission. She needed bed rest and medical monitoring.

No time for that.

She opened her eyes again and looked out at Beirut's ugly concrete outskirts. They had passed the last of the concrete high rises and were coming to a warehouse district.

Boucher drove them to a medium-sized, isolated one behind a chain link fence topped with razor wire. A man in the uniform of a local security company stood in a sentry box at the front gate, a compact submachinegun slung from his shoulder.

"Don't worry," Boucher said. "They know we're coming."

From a nearby shed, two other men emerged, also dressed as security. Jana wondered if this company was real or just another part of the camouflage.

Boucher stopped just before the gate and parked to the side of the driveway.

"From here we walk."

They got out. Two of the guards came over and frisked Jacob and Hervé while the third guard kept watch. Once they were done, one of the guards came over to her. She opened up her jacket to show her shoulder holster. He removed the gun and frisked her anyway.

"Careful with your hands," Jana told him in Arabic.

The guard ignored her and kept frisking. A bit too thoroughly for her liking.

She slapped him upside the head. "I said careful with your hands."

The guard glowered at her but backed off.

Too bad I'm not carrying a holdout. I'd feel better going in there with something.

They opened the gate and Boucher led them inside with an air of someone who had been here a lot. Jana wondered what kind of deals the French were using this smuggling operation for.

Two of the guards accompanied them, walking a bit behind, guns sloped but the hands that held them tense.

They walked to the warehouse under a hot Middle Eastern sun, their footsteps crunching gravel. The giant doors of the loading dock were closed. They passed them and went to a smaller door just around the corner.

Boucher turned to the guards. One of them nodded. He opened the door, and they passed through to a spacious office. Nothing was on the desk, not even a computer. A metal file cabinet stood nearby, no doubt locked. They passed through the office and went to what looked like a break room. A table stood in the center with a few chairs around it. A water dispenser, a small fridge, and a fussball table stood to one side. There was a closed door on the opposite wall.

The guards closed the door to the office.

"We'll wait here," one of them said. "The boss is coming soon, Monsieur Lamartine."

Jana suppressed a smile. Boucher's alias was the same name as one of the most famous French poets of the nineteenth century.

They didn't have long to wait. One of the guard's walkie-talkies crackled.

"He's coming."

"Right," the man transmitted back, without taking his eyes off the three guests.

They heard a door open in the office beyond, then the door to their room opened.

A heavyset Lebanese man, short but with an erect bearing, came through the door. This must be Salim Ibn Omar.

Jana barely focused on him. Because coming through the door right behind him strode a huge man who was half Slav and half Asiatic with a shaved head with a queue reaching past his shoulders and a long, thin scar down one side of his face.

Jana, Jacob, and the newcomer all gasped at the same time.

Because this was ChingisBeshimov, a Kyrgyz killer-for-hire who Jacob had tangled with on a previous mission. Jana had become acquainted with him the last time they had come to Beirut and went to a bar that gun runners and mercenaries frequented.

Chingis had been there, and denounced Jacob as CIA to the entire place. They had barely gotten out of there alive.

The mercenary jabbed a finger in Jacob's direction.

"You! Boss, this man is CIA!"

Things got a bit confused after that.

CHAPTER TWELVE

Aaron Peters was surprised they didn't come for him sooner. He had woken up from his drugged stupor to find himself back in his cell as he expected. His head felt muzzy and he had a nasty rope burn around his neck, not to mention a sore neck.

At least he was alive for the moment. The guards had been shooting to kill, but when he had fallen victim to that trap, they had decided to spare him. Why? Did they really think they could make him turn traitor?

Maybe Dr. Harlow thought they could, or the higher-ups in The Order, but Tyson should know better.

Except Tyson had turned. Aaron would have never guessed he would. No, not in a million years.

Not having anything else to do, Aaron lay down on his bedroll and was soon asleep. He needed to save his energy for whatever would come next.

He must have slept in, because he was startled awake by the opening of his feeding slit.

A tray was shoved through with a bowl of cornflakes, a couple of scrambled eggs, and a banana.

Aaron ate. Nothing happened until noon, when he was given another meal. After that, he didn't see a sign of his captors until dinner, when they fed him again.

He supposed that this silence and return to routine was supposed to rattle him. It didn't. They would do what they would do, and he would have little chance to affect the outcome. His training kept him from letting it get to him.

During this time, he continued to read the thick pile of documents they had given him. While Aaron knew he was being fed propaganda, he wanted to see where The Order and Dr. Harlow were coming from.

And this propaganda was of the trickiest type, for it contained truth. Climate change, pandemics, dwindling resources—all of these problems and the rest they outlined in the documents were certainly threats to global stability. What he couldn't figure out was how much of the data were exaggerated.

The conclusion the report came to was a stark one—that within a decade, two at most, the world would reach a tipping point from which it could not recover. Climate change would aggravate the steady decline in resources to the point of making large-scale regional wars inevitable. This would affect the supply chain, causing further shortages and price hikes and destabilizing more economies. This would lead to more war, and more economic disruption in an ever-accelerating downward spiral.

Something had to be done, and quickly.

The solution his captors had come to wasn't an acceptable one. Even assuming the situation was as bleak as the report laid out, a global tyranny by some shadowy group using ancient technology was an even worse fate for the world. They had killed tens of thousands already. What would they do when the new rulers faced a mass rebellion? Or even a peaceful industrial strike?

These people didn't care about human lives. They were only using the idea of saving the planet as an excuse to grab power. They might not even consciously realize that themselves, and that made them even more dangerous.

History had seen this countless times before on a smaller scale. Dictators always used some sort of national emergency, real or imagined, as an excuse to grab power. But those same dictators only ended up making matters worse in the long run.

These people needed to be stopped, no matter how legitimate their concerns about the planet might be.

The question was—how the hell was he going to stop them?

First, he needed rest. Perhaps the next day would bring him some opportunities.

He slept soundly that night. Too soundly. It was like someone switched a light off in his head and he had no dreams, no partially conscious awareness of sounds or rolling over. He simply switched off.

Aaron barely woke up when they opened his cell door, secured his wrists and ankles, and carried him out of the cell.

They must have drugged my dinner, he thought, the idea coming slowly to his mind, barely formed.

He felt so sluggish he fell asleep on the way, waking up strapped to a chair.

Aaron struggled to focus. When he did, he blinked his eyes, shook his head to try to clear it, and looked around.

He was in a small room with concrete walls measuring about ten feet by ten. He was strapped to a metal chair bolted to the floor right in the middle of the room. In front of him stood Roger Tyson and a man and a woman in lab coats. Turning his head to his left, he could see two guards standing in front of a closed metal door like the one in his cell, assault rifles sloped, the safeties off.

Tyson grinned. "Hey, Aaron. Nice escape attempt. I wasn't around, but I saw the footage. The old 'pretend suicide' trick. I'm surprised these guys fell for it, although you sure made it look convincing. How's the neck? Looks red as hell. Swollen, too."

Aaron glared at him. His former comrade's grin didn't falter.

"Don't judge me, buddy. I'm with the good guys. I know it doesn't feel like that from where you're sitting, but it's true."

"Come on, Tyson. You don't believe that. Look at the body count. You're in it for the money. Or did they offer you something else?"

His old comrade's eyes lit up. "They offered me a better future."

"Never thought you'd sell out."

"I didn't sell out. I bought it. Bought into a new world where we can all live in peace."

"Get real."

"I have gotten real, more real than I ever was stuck in that old life. You know what it's like out there. Every country jockeying for position. Revolutions. Wars. Sure, America and her allies are better than most, but we still leave a damn big bloody trail. What's the point? We'll fall just like every empire falls. Maybe we'll be remembered better than most, a mixed bag like the British Empire, instead of an exploitative mess like the Ottoman Empire, but we'll still fall. All those missions, all that trouble, all that separation from family, for nothing."

Aaron didn't reply. Tyson went on.

"Remember Iraq, Aaron? Remember when we were fighting the insurgency? So many factions in a country most of us had never been to before. Saddam loyalists. Local militias. The Mahdi Army. Al-Qaeda. And a whole bunch more. All operating in cells. No central command to take out. No standing armies to defeat in the field. We'd knock out one unit and another would pop up to cause trouble in a different neighborhood. We'd hit that one, and two more would crop up. Remember that, Aaron? We used to call it Whack-a-Mole, like that old arcade game. No matter how many you knock down, another pops up. Except it was no game. Many of these groups went after their own people even more than they went after us. Settling scores, they couldn't settle when Saddam was in power. God, the things they did! You saw the videos. We all did. Cutting people apart with chainsaws. Pouring buckets of boiling water over them. Cutting their heads off. I never doubted we were on the side of right. Those barbarians needed to be stopped. But I always wondered what was the point of it all. We never stopped them, not really. We could restore something that looked like order in the short term, but it would never last, never be real. Remember that, Aaron?"

Aaron didn't look at him. Yes, he remembered that. All those raids. All that collecting of intel from local informants who all had their own agendas and never told them the full truth. And all these years later, Iraq was still a mess.

Tyson put a hand on his shoulder.

"It's been the same ever since. ISIS. The Taliban. Al-Shabab. Then all the individual actors and nations jockeying for position and making everything worse. Sure, sometimes we win. We break up a drug cartel or stop a suicide bombing. There'd only be another one. On and on until we grow old or get killed, and the new crop of agents has to burn itself out."

Aaron thought of his daughter, pulled into that world against her will. He had trained her, prepared her from a young age to take care of herself, but he had never wanted her to embrace the lifestyle.

And Jacob, who he had brought back from the brink only to throw him into even worse situations than the one he had saved him from.

Those two had always weighed heavily on his heart. They deserved a more peaceful life than what he could give them.

But what could he do? What could anyone do? The world was so full of evil that even if you remained a civilian and pretended none of this was happening, sooner or later that world was going to come after you. Look at all those victims of the hydroelectric dam attacks. Or the civilians caught up in the horror of Islamic State.

Sitting by doing nothing wasn't an option.

But Tyson was right about something. They were all caught on a bloody treadmill with no end in sight.

"Don't you want a break, Aaron? Even you need a break sometimes. Longest covert op in the history of the CIA. I respect that. Who couldn't? But I bet that fishing trip you went on afterwards sure was nice. Maine sure is pretty that time of year."

A memory flashed in Aaron's mind, a memory of an agent who drove him up to that safehouse in Maine. Something he said …

Tyson gave his shoulder a squeeze.

"We can end all that. Oh, sure, I know what you're going to say. Lots of groups have tried to take over the world. None of them ever got close and they all made a bigger mess than what they started with. The Order is different. You see, we have a vision. A technocratic society ruled by science and reason. We'll crush out the tribalism that has plagued humanity, we'll change the shortsighted system that's led to environmental degradation and endless war. We can do it, Aaron. We're different. With Dr. Harlow's help, we've harnessed technology the world hasn't seen in a hundred thousand years. We're going to rebuild the only civilization that ever brought global peace, and we'll do it better than they ever did."

Aaron remembered what he, Jana, and Jacob had learned in Tibet. An old monk had told them about an ancient manuscript he had read when he was young that talked about that great civilization, which the Tibetans called the Ancient Kingdom of Great Wisdom and Folly. It had built cities and powered flying machines with what the Tibetan manuscript had referred to as magic, but which Aaron knew to be high technology. A form of limitless power brought up out of the earth itself had powered it all. The empire had ruled over the globe for countless years, but only in the north and in some outposts along the equator and further south. The rest of humanity lived in primitive circumstances, fearing the great civilization.

Then there had been some internal fight, some sort of civil war, and their power network got cut off. The civilization crumbled and got overrun by the primitive people it had kept on the margins. Now, only traces of this civilization survived.

Traces that Dr. Harlow and others had been meticulously reconstructing.

So Tyson and his bosses thought they wouldn't repeat the same mistakes? Of course they would. It was human nature to. They were as deluded as the Islamists Aaron had fought for so long, thinking that if their own special ideology could only get in a position of power, the world would turn into paradise.

The old delusion. The same as the Communists. The same as the Nazis. We can kill as many as we want, because it would all turn out good in the end.

Well, he wasn't going to fall for it. Aaron was amazed that someone as bright as Tyson had swallowed those tired old lines.

Tyson took a step back, and the man and woman in lab coats approached. The woman gave him an injection while the man strapped his head to the back of the chair so that he couldn't move it. Then he put clamps on Aaron's eyes to keep them open. The cold steel felt like it was jabbing his eyelids. The doctor fixed a pair of bottles to either side of the backrest. Running from them were plastic tubes that dripped fluid into his eyes, keeping them from drying out.

Tyson pulled down a projector screen. Someone hit an unseen button, and Tyson's voice came over a speaker.

"You know what it's like. Every country jockeying for position. Revolutions. Wars. Sure, America and her allies are better than most, but we still leave a damn big bloody trail. What's the point? … "

Tyson's lecture began to play back to him. The screen lit up with charts and graphs. Deforestation. Microplastic content in fish. Projections of when the world would run out of fossil fuels.

"Sorry for being so overly dramatic," Tyson said over the sound of his own recorded voice, "but it's going to help you see sense. You've read all the facts, heard all the arguments, but your training is holding you back from accepting the truth. That shot they've given you will help open your eyes. It's not mind control, but more mind opening. You'll see."

The guards opened the door, and everyone walked out. Straining his eyes to the left, he could just see them.

"We'll leave you here for a while. Try to relax. The drug will take effect soon. But that's not what's going to change your mind, Aaron. The facts will. See you soon, buddy."

The door closed, and a heavy bolt snapped into place.

Aaron felt his muscles relax. His mind began to empty of thoughts.

He balled his hands into fists, flexing his muscles, but after a moment he forgot to expend the energy and they relaxed again. He clenched again, and then relaxed quicker this time.

After the third attempt, he forgot to make a fourth.

He tried to keep focused, run through memories and plans in his head to keep his mind occupied.

Those thoughts drifted away, and all he could hear was Tyson's lecture, and all he could see were those charts coming up one after another on the screen …

CHAPTER THIRTEEN

Jacob knew he was in trouble the instant he saw ChingisBeshimov come through the door. The Kyrgyz let out a roar and pulled out a pair of UZIs.

Jacob had dealt with Chingis before, and had a sneaking suspicion that "Overkill" was his middle name. That guy was going to spray the entire break room with bullets, taking out him, Jana, Boucher, and probably a few of the guards as well.

Chingis didn't care. He had a bloodlust for Jacob. Something to do with that knife scar Jacob had given him across his face a few years back. He held a grudge for some reason. An unhealthy obsession. Maybe he should get therapy.

Jacob decided that getting sprayed with bullets wasn't how he wanted to finish the day, so as the man mountain drew his guns, Jacob tossed a chair at his head. That was all the therapy Chingis would get from him.

The chair crashed against the killer's skull, making him stagger back. Any other man would have been floored, but not ChingisBeshimov. Jacob threw himself across the room and tackled the guy.

That did the trick. They both went down, the sound of the UZIs going off jabbing in his ears. They stitched twin lines in the ceiling, taking out one of the fluorescent lights and sending a snowfall of particles from the ceiling panels.

As soon as they both hit the floor, Jacob shifted and got his legs onto the Kyrgyz's arms, pinning them. The psycho didn't stop shooting, though, and one of the guards went down with a bullet in the foot.

Jacob heard the sounds of fighting all around him, the snap of a pistol shot, and the crash of furniture.

He didn't have time to look. Chingis bucked like an unbroken stallion and nearly threw him off. Jacob held on for dear life, keeping his legs on the guy's arms and clamping down with both hands on his opponent's wrists to keep him from maneuvering his guns to point at him.

This wasn't going well. While he managed to keep from getting cut apart by a pair of UZIs, the Kyrgyz bucked and thrashed. It was all Jacob could do to keep him on the floor. He couldn't disarm him; he couldn't even move or look away. He was a sitting duck to Ibn Omar or any of the guards.

Just then, one of the guards fell on him. Not tackled, but fell, screaming and holding his face from some blow by one of Jacob's colleagues.

That did the worst possible thing—it knocked Jacob right off of Chingis. With startling speed, Chingis whipped around, got on his knees, and aimed both UZIs at Jacob's head.

Jacob pushed the guard at Chingis and the man jerked a little dance as the bullets meant for Jacob hit the guard instead.

Jacob rolled to the side and lashed out with a foot, connecting perfectly on the Kyrgyz killer's chin.

That knocked him silly. Jacob didn't flatter himself, though. Even that hard of a kick wouldn't take out a man like Chingis for long.

Jacob took a half-second survey of the room and saw Jana lashing out with a chair as a guard tried to gut her with a knife. Not far off, Boucher used his belt like a whip, slicing open a guard's arm far more than the belt buckle should. Was there a razor hidden in there?

The guy who had fallen on him must have been a victim of that. He was still on the ground, clutching his face. Jacob tried to pull the pistol out of his holster.

The guard, although blinded, could still feel the move and twisted to keep Jacob from getting it. Jacob slugged him and went for it again.

Then, the one person he hadn't caught sight of got into the action.

Salim Ibn Omar proved he was more than just a middle-aged businessman by smacking down on Jacob with a heavy glass ashtray he had snatched from the table.

It would have knocked Jacob out if he hadn't gone for that gun. Just at the last second, he shifted position, and instead of hitting him in the back of the head, the ashtray struck him on the shoulder blade.

Jacob grunted and fell to the floor. The guard rolled away. Jacob flipped over, took another blow from the ashtray to the forearm, then kicked the smuggler in the nuts.

That took care of that problem, just in time for Jacob to be faced with another one.

Chingis had woken up from that kick to the jaw and was scrambling for his guns.

Jacob slugged him, and got a backhand in return that laid him flat. Damn, that guy was strong. It felt like getting hit by a baseball bat if baseball bats were made of stone. Maybe one of those Roman columns Jana was always talking about. They came in three types. What were they again? Doric something something.

His mind was wandering. He tried to pull himself back into full consciousness.

When he finally raised his head and got his eyes to focus, he saw an UZI turning to point in his direction.

Before he could kick out with his feet, before he could even think to, Boucher's belt lashed Chingis's hand. The Kyrgyz cried out, blood spurting from the back of his hand, and the UZI fell to the floor.

That was the only invitation Jacob needed. With one hand he slugged Chingis, which felt a bit like hitting one of those Roman pillars, and with the other he went for the UZI.

That didn't work too well. Like those Roman pillars, punching Chingis didn't have much of an effect, and so when Jacob's other hand grabbed the UZI, one of Chingis's giant paws clamped down on it.

They struggled for a moment. Boucher lashed the Kyrgyz on the back, making him cry out but not budging him an inch.

Then Chingis got the upper hand, wrenching the gun from Jacob. Boucher whipped him again, and this time Jacob saw the razor blade poking out from beneath the belt buckle. A line of blood erupted from Chingis's wrist, and he dropped the UZI again.

Just then, there was a complication. Salim ibn Omar got over the kick to the balls enough to grab one of the walkie-talkies.

"All guards to the break room!"

Granted he did sound a bit on the high end of soprano and he was still curled up on the floor, but he had just made their situation a whole lot worse.

Nothing Jacob could do about that now except try to get that UZI. The second one was somewhere out of sight and since Chingis wasn't looking for it, neither would he. He didn't have the time.

Both men dove for the weapon.

Boucher's belt came down again, snapping against the UZI and making it fly several feet across the floor. He sure was good with that thing. Did they train with razor belts in French spy school?

Chingis scrambled for it, and Jacob grabbed him, hauling him back like an oversized fish. Chingis kicked free, got another lash across the back, and dove for the UZI.

He grabbed it, rolled, and got up, ready to fire.

Only to have to duck again when Jana shot at him from across the room, using a pistol she must have taken from the guard lying unconscious amid the remnants of a chair at her feet.

Her shot planted itself in the wall near his head, and he replied with a burst that sent her diving behind the heavy table. It also sent Boucher and Jacob flying in opposite directions.

Jacob rolled, came across the other UZI, and grabbed it.

Chingis may have been as barbaric as his namesake Genghis Khan, but he was also as wily as him too. He saw which way the fight was going and, spraying the room to keep everyone ducking and dodging, rushed out the door.

Or, to be more accurate, through the door. He simply slammed his way through, the cheap plywood shattering.

Jacob turned and aimed at Salim ibn Omar, who was just getting to his feet, holding his arm as blood ran through his fingers from a flesh wound.

"Not so fast," Jacob told him. "Hey, Chingis! You forgot your boss! In fact, I think you shot him, you big dummy."

Just then, a grenade rolled into the room. Jacob dove for cover, not finding much on this side of the room. He ended up lying behind a dead body. That might work.

There was a loud bang, not as loud as a fragmentation or stun grenade, followed by a sharp hiss.

Thick orange smoke billowed out of the grenade, filling the room within a matter of moments.

CHAPTER FOURTEEN

Jana coughed as the smoke reached her. It wasn't teargas, just regular smoke, but bad enough to make her eyes run and her lungs cry out for clean air.

Suddenly, her head was throbbing. This had happened before, right after her injury, when she got out of breath through exertion. Now she was coughing her lungs out and that created the same effect.

She needed to get out of here. Fast.

Jana remembered the door on her end of the long room, opposite from the one through which that crazy Kyrgyz man had fled. Praying it was unlocked, she headed for it.

She heard coughing from the other end of the room. A shot rang out. Jana didn't have time to think about the others. If she didn't get out of there, she'd fall unconscious and end up being a liability. As much as it made her feel guilty to think it, Jacob and Boucher would have to fend for themselves.

Stumbling into the far wall, she groped around, skull pulsing, lungs heaving, until she found the doorknob. To her relief, it opened, and she spilled out into a large warehouse. The lights were on but she didn't see anyone, just long rows of shelves and some palettes with wooden crates.

Jana ended up on her hands and knees, crawling away from the door to get to some fresh air.

Her lungs sucked in oxygen and her coughing subsided, but the throbbing in her head continued, regular pulses of pain that almost made her fall on her face.

Jana was too weak to do anything except remain there on her hands and knees, breathing in fresh air and hoping her head would stop feeling like a series of internal explosions were trying to shatter her skull.

She realized she had dropped her gun. When? Back in the room or afterwards?

Another shot rang out. Jana turned to face the door and fell on her rear. Sitting there, she blearily looked around and didn't see her pistol.

Smoke billowed out of the door. She coughed again, and felt a lightning pain in her head. Jana crawled further away.

Her coughing stopped after she made it to clear air again. Her head kept pounding, though. She struggled to stand, holding onto one of the heavy steel shelves to do so.

The sound of a door opening somewhere in the warehouse made her spin around. That nearly sent her to the floor. Gasping with breath, wincing from the pain in her head, she moved a few steps further down the aisle to hide herself behind all the boxes on the shelves.

The sound of running footsteps. A guard came into view, holding an AK-47. He stopped at the door, his back to Jana, trying to peer through the thick cloud. A shout and another shot came from within.

The guard didn't know what to do. He couldn't tell friend from foe, so he took up position to one side of the doorway, leveled his gun, and waited.

He still hadn't seen Jana peeking around the boxes that hid her.

Jana knew her luck wouldn't last. She needed to get rid of this guy before one of her friends came out that door. She could hear them coughing in there, struggling with someone. Further away, she could hear shouting. Chingis was gathering reinforcements.

And what if more came around to this side? She needed to get that AK.

Jana looked around for some sort of weapon, a box cutter or a wrench or something. All she saw were boxes. Her head still throbbed, but the pain was manageable now that her lungs had cleared.

The break room was clearing too. The smoke in there, billowing out of both open doors, was quickly thinning. In a few more seconds the figures inside would become visible and that guy, and the guards at the other door, would start shooting.

Jana didn't feel up to a fight, but she had no choice.

She hefted some of the smaller boxes, trying not to make any noise. She found one small one that was filled with something heavy and solid. She picked it up and moved down the aisle toward her target.

Just as she came into view, she saw a figure emerge from the smoke, bent over and coughing. The guard hiding around the side of the door heard the footsteps and raised his AK-47.

Jana threw the box at him with all her might.

The effort made her head throb with pain, and she stumbled. Her aim was good enough, though. While she had gone for the head, the box ended up hitting him in the waist. The force and surprise made him jerk, and his shot went into the ceiling.

Boucher came out, coughing and holding that belt fitted with a razor on the buckle. His eyes were tearing, his lungs heaving, but he had enough sense left to rush in the direction of that shot and slam into the guard.

Both went down. The AK dropped from the criminal's hand.

Jana rushed for it, her steps clumsy.

The guard recovered first, grabbing the gun and trying to get to his feet. Boucher lashed out with a fist, barely able to see, and landed a punch in his gut. That stopped the guard from firing long enough that Jana made it there and clocked him one across the jaw.

She had a perfect target and would normally have laid this guy flat, but her punch was weak. All it achieved was to snap his head back and make him focus on her.

He slammed the assault rifle into her chest and she staggered back, cartwheeling her arms to keep from falling. She couldn't afford to hit her head again. The guard leveled the gun at her.

Boucher rose, grabbing the gun and deflecting it just as the guard fired. A bullet panged off the metal shelving next to Jana. Boucher and the guard struggled a moment. Jacob emerged coughing from the room with Salim ibn Omar in a headlock. Seeing the situation, he kicked the smuggler to the floor and joined Boucher as he struggled with the guard for control of the gun.

Neither of her companions had one. That was going to be a problem really damn soon. She hurried over to Salim ibn Omar, gave him a punch to keep him down, and searched his pockets. Other than a fat wallet, a cell phone, and some keys, he had nothing.

By the time she turned back to Jacob and Boucher, she found the guard laid out on the floor with blood flowing from a blow to the head, and Jacob with his hands on the AK-47. Boucher still only had that deadly belt of his.

Jacob turned to her. "We need to—"

Whatever he said got drowned out by a hail of fire coming from the break room. The smoke had cleared to a light haze, and Chingis and a couple of other guards swept the room with bullets.

Several came through the door to hit the shelving beyond.

Jana hunkered down to one side of the door guarding Salim ibn Omar while Jacob knelt by the doorway and returned fire. Boucher ran off into the warehouse.

For a minute there was stalemate, both sides trading shots but neither scoring a hit. Then another grenade rolled through the doorway. Jana grabbed it and tossed it back. It detonated with a sharp bang and once again the room filled with smoke.

That gave them a moment. Chingis had obviously wanted to smoke out this part of the warehouse and make a charge. Instead, he had blocked his own advance.

Now he'd probably send most of the guards around to cut off their retreat, while leaving one man to cover the break room.

They needed to get out of here. Fast.

Jana lifted the smuggler by the shoulders and started to drag him away from the door, through which a few shots still sang. Her head pulsed with pain at the effort, but a bullet would probably hurt a whole lot more. Jacob let out a burst through the break room and withdrew too. Being on opposite sides of the door, they ended up retreating down different aisles of the warehouse. The aisles ran a good forty feet. Jana didn't like being separated like this.

She kept dragging Ibn Omar, her strength beginning to flag before she even made it halfway down the aisle. The firing from the other end of the break room died down.

Jana's hands slipped and Ibn Omar thumped to the floor. She leaned against the steel shelves, her breath ragged. Just a few seconds to rest. That's all she'd give herself.

A shot rang out. It sounded clear and close.

Inside the warehouse.

Jana cursed and lifted up the smuggler again, dragging him down the aisle and nearly tripping over her own feet.

She heard a shout that sounded like Boucher, followed by running feet. Jana kept looking over her shoulder as she dragged her heavy burden backwards down the aisle. She was an easy target here.

Her breath caught as someone jumped into view at the end of the aisle. She let out a sigh of relief to see it was Boucher.

Now he was carrying an AK-47. His belt was back on, dribbling blood down the front of his trousers.

"Where did you get that?" she managed to gasp as she continued dragging the smuggler. Damn, this guy was heavy.

"Killed a guard. Jacob is covering the only entrance. We need to go."

He rushed up and took one of Salim ibn Omar's arms. Together they dragged him down the rest of the aisle and to a clear space. Not far off stood an open doorway, a dead guard nearby. Jacob knelt by the entrance, peering down the barrel of his captured gun.

Salim ibn Omar groaned and tried to struggle. Boucher kicked him.

"Stay silent if you know what's good for you."

He wouldn't have been heard anyway, because just then several shots rang out from outside the warehouse. Jacob ducked back as the doorframe splintered.

"Chingis and a couple of guys are out there," Jacob said when the firing died down. "Hiding behind a van."

"When the smoke clears in the break room, they'll come at us from behind," Jana said.

Jacob pointed at the smuggler. "Get him over here. Time to cut a deal."

Boucher, seeing how exhausted Jana was, handed her his gun and dragged ibn Omar over to the doorway.

"Hey, Chingis!" Jacob shouted. "We have your boss hostage. We're leaving with him. You cause any trouble, and we'll blow his brains out."

Jacob didn't mean that. He had never killed a helpless man in his life. Jana sure hoped Chingis didn't call his bluff.

Jana heard some angry words she took to be Kyrgyz swear words, then a question in Arabic.

"You have him? I want to see him."

Jacob nodded, and Boucher dragged the half-conscious smuggler into view, being careful to use the portly man as a shield. Jana sidled up to the door in case he needed cover fire.

She darted a look out and saw a van parked about twenty yards away. She could see a couple of other men peeking around the edge of it.

"All right," Chingis called. "You got a lot more trouble on your hands than you realize. You know this man's family?"

"I do," Boucher replied.

"Then you know the kind of vengeance they'll bring on your heads for kidnapping him."

"Better than staying here," Jacob replied. "You going to give us safe passage or not?"

Long pause.

"Looks like we don't have much choice," Chingis growled.

"All right. We're going to move back through the building to where we came in. Then we're passing through the gate and getting into our car. Any funny business, and your boss gets one in the head."

Chingis whispered something to his companions.

"All right," he called back.

"I don't trust him," Jana whispered.

"You shouldn't," Jacob whispered back.

"All right," Jacob called to him. "We're moving out now. I don't want to see any of your men on the way out. Deal?"

Pause.

"Deal."

Jacob nodded, and they moved back away from the door.

As Jana covered their retreat, Boucher led a more conscious and cowed Salim ibn Omar down one of the aisles as Jacob took point. They checked the break room, found it clear, and Jacob rushed ahead to the office beyond. Boucher followed with the prisoner. Jana held her breath as she passed through the lingering smoke, but that made her head hurt too. She got to the office and was grateful to see the door to the outside already open and fresh air blowing in.

Still, when she finally took a breath, she caught some smoke and let out a little cough, accompanied by a jab of pain in her head.

Not now. I can't afford this now.

Jacob peeked out the door.

"I don't see anyone," he whispered.

"That means nothing," Boucher said. "Ah!"

He led the prisoner over to a dead guard, whom he relieved of a sidearm.

"Looks better now, eh?" he said with a grin, pointing the gun at the smuggler's head.

"I see you put your belt back on," Jacob said. "Quite the fashion accessory."

"A Frenchman should always be well dressed."

"Is that dribble of half-dried blood down your crotch the latest Parisian fashion?"

Jana coughed again, eliciting another spike of pain. "Can we stop joking around and get out of here, please?"

The two men looked at her, and their expressions made her heart sink. Even the smuggler with a gun to his head looked shocked.

"Are you OK?" Jacob and Boucher asked unison.

"Yes. No. Let's go."

Another cough. Another spike of pain.

Jacob called out the doorway. “We’re coming out. No one try anything.”

Boucher went first, using Salim ibn Omar as a shield and keeping a gun to his head. Jana came next, almost getting in front of them just to get out of that smoky room before remembering that their prisoner was their only chance of escape. Jacob took up the rear.

The fresh air revived her a little. Only a little. She walked wearily, barely able to keep her AK-47 raised. Looking around, she didn’t see anyone. Had Chingis really decided to keep his word?

The crack of a shot and the buzz of a nearby bullet told her he hadn’t.

CHAPTER FIFTEEN

Jacob cursed and spun around, firing a quick, unaimed shot at the corner of the building just as a figure ducked back out of sight.

"Try that again and I'll blow his brains out!" Boucher shouted.

They heard Chingis laugh. "No, you won't. You're CIA. You're not allowed."

"You idiots!" Salim ibn Omar shouted. "If you start a gunfight, I'll get killed by a stray bullet. Stay back, that's an order!"

Silence. They continued for the car. Jana felt keyed up and dizzy. She kept having to turn as she walked, looking all around her—at both corners of the building, at the door, at the car they were trying to get to. There could be threats anywhere. She had to keep vigilant, and yet each time she turned her stomach felt queasy and her head ached.

They made it without further incident, Jana collapsing more than sitting in the passenger's seat. No way was she fit to drive. Jacob shot her a concerned look and got behind the wheel, Boucher and the prisoner getting in back.

Jacob took off to a squeal of tires. Jana opened the window in case she needed to fire. The hot breeze wafting in her face revived her somewhat. Sitting down helped too.

Jacob darted a glance at her. "Did you get hurt back there?"

"No."

"You're as white as a sheet."

"It's just … that old injury."

"Damn," Jacob muttered. "We'll have it looked at when we can."

When we can.

Like we'll ever have time on this mission.

Boucher looked out the rear window. "They're following us."

Jana looked in the rearview mirror rather than turn her sensitive head, and saw a van and a four-by-four following them about fifty yards back. Jacob sped up, getting on an access road to the highway and passing the few vehicles in sight. The van began to lag behind, but the four-by-four kept pace.

"I'll bet you a thousand bucks Chingis is driving that," Jacob said.

"I won't take that bet," Jana replied.

"How do you know my chief bodyguard?" Salim ibn Omar asked.

"Oh, we go way back. Best of buddies," Jacob said, swerving around another vehicle and picking up more speed.

"What do we do?" Jana asked. "We got to lose him but I bet he's an even crazier driver than you."

Jacob grinned. "Me? Crazy driver? What are you talking about?"

He swerved off the access road and up a gritty slope toward the highway.

"Take the on ramp, you idiot!" Salim ibn Omar said.

"Why? This is more fun."

Jana put on her seatbelt.

"He's driving a four-by-four," Boucher said. "You're not going to shake him that way."

"No. I'll shake him this way."

Jacob thumped onto the highway and swerved through three lanes of traffic.

"Sacre bleu!"

They left a chorus of squealing tires and honks in their wake. Chingis got onto the highway, too, swerving through traffic. He cut one driver off to close and the guy swerved, sideswiping another vehicle. Both barely maintained control.

"You're going to cause collateral damage," Boucher said.

"Hm. Good point. We'll have to lose him another way."

Jacob cut across two lanes and got onto an off ramp. A pickup truck filled with cabbages was going forty in front of them. The off ramp was narrow with guardrails to either side. There was nowhere to go.

The four-by-four roared right up behind them. Just as she feared, Jana could see Chingis at the wheel, an evil grin on his face. Another guard sat next to him.

"They better not fire," Salim ibn Omar muttered, as if to himself.

"I hope you pay these guys well," Jana said.

"Don't you know?" the smuggler snapped. "You've obviously been spying on me."

Boucher rapped the pistol barrel against his head. "You know why we're here."

"No, I don't."

"The medical shipment to the Syrian People's Front."

"They were rebuilding hospitals."

"Cut the crap," Jacob said.

Chingis was still right behind them. Salim ibn Omar smiled.

"Or what will you do exactly?"

"You're not going to get away," Jana said, "and that raging barbarian behind us is not going to save you. Tell us what we want to know if you ever want to see the outside of a prison cell."

The smuggler chuckled. "You obviously don't know much about Lebanese politics."

"You obviously don't know much about CIA politics," Jana shot back. "You think your connections in the government will help you? You think you can bribe a Lebanese judge so you can walk free? Well, you'd be right if you got to stay in Lebanon. But we're taking you out of the country."

"That's illegal!"

"So is smuggling bioweapons," Jacob said.

"Bioweapons? I know of no bioweapons."

Boucher rapped his pistol barrel against his head again. "Don't play stupid."

The pickup truck finally got onto a two-lane side road, and Jacob could speed past it. Chingis came right behind them. He didn't try to ram them, and his comrade didn't lean out the window to shoot. They held back because their boss was captive. Chingis was crazy though, and Jana wondered how long he would be able to control himself.

They were approaching a built-up area, getting out of the warehouse and industrial district and back to the suburbs, marked by rows of dreary concrete tower blocks. At the street level were shops and plenty of traffic.

"You're never going to lose him here," Salim ibn Omar said with a smile.

"You don't know who's at the wheel," Jana told him.

Jacob swerved off onto a side road between the tower blocks. He couldn't drive fast because there was traffic here and people crossing the street. Chingis kept right behind them.

Another stalemate. Chingis didn't dare fire, and Jacob couldn't shake him. Jana wondered why he had chosen to get on this busy residential street.

She figured it out a minute later when he swerved onto an empty part of the sidewalk, crashing through a park and taking out a couple of bushes along the way before driving in between two of the tower blocks.

It was a narrow lane, just barely wide enough for Chingis to get his four-by-four through as he roared after them, but Jana saw what her lover was planning when they came across a series of heavy metal dumpsters lining one side of the lane.

Jacob moved the car as far to the left as possible, the sideview mirror plinking off and a terrible scraping sound coming all along the vehicle's left side.

"My government is very stingy about expenses," Boucher said.

"How about funeral services?" Jacob asked.

"A bit more generous, but let's just ruin the car."

Even as far left as they got, the right side of the car still scraped against the dumpsters and they lost the other sideview mirror.

The terrible sound of screeching metal lasted only for a few seconds and then they were past.

A loud crash behind them signaled Chingis trying and failing to get through. Jana looked at the rearview mirror and saw the four-by-four jammed up between the wall and the dumpsters. With a screech of metal, it backed up, then Chingis revved the engine and slammed into the dumpster with full force. The heavy metal bins bucked, trash flying out of them, but they barely moved a couple of feet. Chingis pulled back for a second try.

"It won't be long before his lizard brain figures out that he should go around," Jana said. "Step on it!"

Jacob stepped on it, crashing through a fruit stand on the opposite road and smearing the car with crushed oranges as he swerved onto another road and hit the gas, weaving between cars. He took the first turn he came to, ended up on a parallel road lined with tower blocks, then took another turn to speed away from the area.

Jana turned around in the seat, careful not to move her head too quickly, and didn't see any sign of Chingis. She did hear a police siren in the distance, though.

"Whoops," Jacob said. "I'll get on the highway and merge with the rest of the traffic."

"You can't merge with traffic with scrapes along both sides of the car, both sideview mirrors gone, and covered in fruit pulp," Jana pointed out.

"Oh. Right. Guess we better ditch it."

"That means ditching the weapons."

"I can keep the pistol," Boucher said.

"Yes, but you're going to wrap my jacket around your waist so people don't think you've wet your pants with blood," Jana said.

"But it's a woman's jacket!"

Jana rolled her eyes. That sounded like something Jacob would say. Were all these male operatives the same? She was beginning to think so.

Jacob drove until he found an isolated patch of waste ground behind a construction site and ditched the car. Boucher took Jana's jacket with a grumble and covered up his bloodstains. They began to walk. Jacob and Boucher walked on either side of their prisoner, who was looking around him, obviously thinking how he could escape. Jana trailed wearily behind. They could still hear police sirens in the distance.

"We need to get back into central Beirut," Jacob said.

"How?" Jana asked. The sun shone strong and while the pain in her head had subsided, she worried a long walk in the sun would bring it back.

Boucher pulled out his phone. "I'll call an Uber."

"You want to call an Uber when we have one of Lebanon's leading smugglers at gunpoint?" Jana said.

The Frenchman shrugged. "Better than the bus."

"We could steal a car," Jacob suggested.

"The police are already on the alert," Boucher said. "It's better if we take an Uber. Hey! There's one just a few blocks away."

"I can't believe this," Jana said.

Boucher tapped on his screen. "He's coming. So convenient. Don't worry. I've transported prisoners on Uber before. We'll just pretend to be tourists with a Lebanese host."

Jacob looked around. "In this neighborhood?"

"OK. We work for a construction company that's supplying wiring to that building site we ditched the car behind. You got that, Salim? You're going to play along, otherwise I'll use the belt on you. Now let's get cleaned up before the Uber gets here."

"I can't believe this," Jana muttered, wiping the dust off her clothing as well as she could.

CHAPTER SIXTEEN

The Uber driver greeted them with the usual effusive, chatty welcome of anyone in the Middle East meeting foreigners who actually spoke the language. That began to die as he sensed the tension in the car, saw Jana's pallor, and Salim ibn Omar's sullenness.

Jana sat in the passenger's seat, trying to keep up a conversation with the man to put him at ease, while Jacob and Boucher sat in the back, on either side of a stony-faced ibn Omar.

After a few blocks, the driver stopped talking at all and kept his eyes fixed on the road. He had gone into avoidance mode, another Middle Eastern reaction. Something was going on that he didn't understand, and so he pretended not to see it in the hope that it wouldn't end up involving him. His country had been through too much for the average Lebanese to stick their noses in other people's business.

They had him drop them downtown in a busy shopping district near the seaside, and from there they walked a couple of blocks, casting nervous glances at a pair of policemen walking their beat, until they could hail a cab to take them to another part of town close to one of Boucher's safehouses.

Now reasonably assured that they wouldn't be followed, they got the smuggler inside and strapped him to a chair with some rope the French agent had handy. Boucher went to the bedroom to change his trousers. He kept spare clothing in all of the safehouses, he explained.

"Although I'm going to have to take all this away," he groaned. "I have a nice suit here I don't want to lose. We've compromised this place by bringing him here."

"We didn't have a choice," Jana said.

"And I've lost a government vehicle," Boucher muttered from the bedroom. "Paris is going to be furious with me."

"Sorry," Jana said, nudging her boyfriend. "Anyone who hangs out with this guy ends up regretting it."

"Hey! I'm a great guy to work with."

"You're a mobile disaster area."

Jacob chuckled, then turned grim as he leaned forward to get into Salim ibn Omar's space.

"Time to learn what the Syrian People's Front is up to."

"I don't know anything," the smuggler said.

"You ever been to the Andes, Salim?" Jana asked.

"The Andes?"

"Guantanamo Bay became too famous, so the CIA has opened another detention center high in the Andes of Peru," Jana told him. "I've been there. The prison is at 4,000 meters. Even in summer there's snow on the ground and you can see your breath. The cells are made of concrete and unheated. Sure, you get blankets, but not enough. You'll never be really warm. The food they serve is cold, too. No hot soup to warm your insides."

"And the winters? Damn," Jacob said, picking up Jana's cue. "It gets to minus 40. The wind howls down those peaks like a vengeful ghost. You won't want to be in the yard then. Of course, you only get one hour in the yard anyway. The rest of the time you're in your cell. No windows. No reading material. No mail."

"Only the worst prisoners go there," Jana said. "Those that helped terrorists. And they're all mixed up together. You'll be in there with Shiites."

That, even more that the description of a very un-Middle-Eastern climate, put a look of worry on the smuggler's face.

"You can't do this," he whispered.

Jacob let out a nasty chuckle, obviously enjoying the story Jana had made up. "We're the bad guys, remember? We're the ones that introduced crack to America and invented AIDS in a lab. We do whatever the hell we want, unless we get what we want."

"A-and if I tell you?"

Jana raised an eyebrow. "Tell us what?"

"Whatever you need to know. What if I cooperate?"

"Then we hand you over to the Lebanese authorities."

A spark of hope lit Salim ibn Omar's eyes. That and a heavy dose of calculation.

Boucher walked into the room, adjusting his newly cleaned belt. "Only after we confirm what you said is true."

The smuggler looked from one to the other, thinking.

"Well … " Jana made an encouraging gesture. "Go on."

"Or it's the icebox for you," Jacob said.

The smuggler thought for a moment, looking at each of his captors in turn. Jana tried to keep a poker face. She'd never been very good at lies. It was essential that this scumbag believed it, though.

At last, he let out a big sigh.

"All right. If you promise to hand me over to Lebanese authorities, I will tell you what you want to know."

"It's a deal," Jacob said.

"General Tariq al-Rashid has been my regular customer. Of all the factions in Syria, I only do business with him."

He paused.

Jana gave him an encouraging nod. So far, he was telling the truth. They knew this through Boucher's intel. That was a good sign.

Salim ibn Omar grimaced and went on.

"You should not be going against him. He's a patriot. An Arab patriot."

"How so?"

"He wants to rebuild the old Arab civilization. Take it back to what it once was in its days of medieval greatness, when we were a center of learning and culture."

Boucher snorted. The smuggler gave him a haughty look.

"You think it's silly? Look at the other factions in Syria. The government is a bloodthirsty dictatorship. The Kurds only care about their own interests. The Free Syrian Army is rife with corruption. The Islamists want to ruin all that is good in the world. But General al-Rashid … " the smuggler's eyes took on a bright, faraway look " … General al-Rashid is a visionary."

"A visionary?" Jana said. "You know he's a major drug smuggler, right?"

Ibn Omar spat. "So what? Making money off of decadent Westerners who would rather wreck their bodies and minds than take advantage of all the opportunities their rich nations offer them? They deserve everything they get." He leaned forward as far as his bonds would allow. "And the more we weaken you, the more we will get strong."

Jana realized she had miscalculated. This man was probably a big part of the general's drug operation. She was looking forward to sending in the Lebanese police. While he might be able to bribe his way out of a prison term, the government would confiscate everything he had for themselves.

Haughty now, Salim ibn Omar went on. “The general is leading the Arabs to victory. You haven’t met him. I have. He is an amazing man, a natural leader who cares for his people. He sees through the factionalism you and the Jews created. Syrian against Iraqi. One Bedouin tribe against another. A thousand political and religious parties. He will bring all of us together under the banner of pan-Arab nationalism. And once we unite, we will be as great as the days of the old Caliphs.”

Jana saw an in.

She let out a condescending laugh.

“Unite the Arabs? He can’t even unite Syria! He only runs a fifth of the country. He’s using up all his energy just to hold his territory.”

Ibn Omar stuck out his chin. “Not for long. He has something to tip the balance.”

Silence.

When the smuggler didn’t speak, Boucher cut in. “You mean the bioweapons technology you shipped? We know all about that.”

“I shipped hospital supplies.”

“And laboratory supplies to replicate diseases.”

“Nonsense.” Ibn Omar looked away.

Boucher held up his phone with a grin. “We’ll find out everything we want on this, I bet. We have a team right here in Beirut that can crack this like an egg and serve up the intel to us for breakfast. Plus, remember, if you don't talk, or if you say something that doesn't correlate with what we already know or what we find out on here, then you'll be sneezing out ice cubes in the Andes for the rest of your life."

Again, that calculating look, this time at his phone. Jana imagined that he was wondering just how much could be traced on that device. He was probably thinking back on all the conversations, all his movements, all the photos he had received, and what kind of court case that would add up to.

“All right,” he said with a sigh. “It doesn’t matter. You’re too late.” He grinned at them and laughed. “Do you hear me, you filthy Westerners? You’re too late!”

CHAPTER SEVENTEEN

Aaron felt sluggish and sleepy, and yet sleep would not come. Despite being kept for hours in that damn room watching and listening to propaganda, he was left with a strange restlessness. When they had returned him to his cell, he saw they had done a bit of remodeling.

The entire cell—walls, floor, and ceiling—had been painted in a bizarre pattern of lines and swirls. They almost made shapes, but shapes he could not quite make out. He formed his hands into a circle and looked through it, thinking that seeing only a part of the pattern might reveal if it actually depicted something. He still couldn't figure anything out.

Then he noticed a noise, a soft rustling. At first, he thought it might be a rat. Looking around and pulling the blankets off the floor, he couldn't find one. Then he realized the sound seemed to be coming from all directions.

What was it? He stood still and focused. It was at just the edge of his hearing. Even so, he could make out a cadence to it. After a moment, he realized it was human speech.

Aaron nodded. Subliminal messages. Those patterns on the wall were probably designed to confuse his brain or slip him into some sort of hypnotic state.

He chuckled and laid himself out on the blankets, closing his eyes. Subliminal messaging had been debunked years ago. Advertisers had tried it in commercials back in the Seventies and Eighties. They had never gotten any concrete results and had eventually dropped the idea. The CIA didn't use it in any of their interrogation practices.

Maybe they've discovered some ancient technique.

The idea actually made Aaron laugh out loud. He imagined talking to his daughter,

"Sorry, kiddo. I've been brainwashed into joining The Order using a technique developed by that pre-Ice Age civilization you don't believe in. I got hypnotized by ghosts."

He'd get a hell of an eye roll for that one.

The voice kept speaking, just on the edge of hearing.

Then his feeding slit snapped open and a plastic tray scraped across the floor.

Dinner. Or was it lunch? Chicken fillet, already going cold, with a side of green beans, plus an orange and a paper cup of water. Not exactly *haute cuisine*, but it would keep him alive.

He reached for it and hesitated. What if it was drugged like his last meal?

Well, what if it was? If they wanted to dose him with something, he couldn't stop them. If he refused to eat, they'd simply come in and give him an injection. He could use that as a chance to attack, but they'd be more careful this time. They might even inject a gas through the feeding slit.

Aaron grimaced as he looked at the food. There was no way he could avoid being subjected to whatever drugs they wanted, so he might as well eat.

He ate, the pattern of lines and swirls on the walls of his cell making his eyes feel strange, unfocused. Eventually, he closed them and ate blind.

Nothing tasted different, but then again it wouldn't, would it?

He finished his meal, shoved the tray over to the feeding slit so the guard could retrieve it, and did some calisthenics. That voice was still talking, and those strange lines were dazzling his eyes. He closed them and went to bed.

Sleep wouldn't come. The voice continued to drone on with its unheard words trying to ease into his subconscious, and even though his eyes were closed he could still see those lines in his mind's eye.

He tried to relax and will sleep to come, first by relaxing the muscles in his feet, then working his way up to his legs, gut, chest, and all the way up to his head. An old technique to use in the field when the time to sleep was dictated by circumstances and not fatigue.

It worked. Too quickly. He felt his mind clear and his body feel like it was floating away.

Damn, they drugged my ...

The voice grew louder, words becoming clear and yet still unheard. The lines all around him began to convulse and shift.

***

“You’re too late!” Salim ibn Omar cackled from where he was tied to a chair in a safehouse of the French secret service. “It doesn’t matter if I tell you everything or not. You’re too late!”

“Then tell us everything,” Jacob said. This guy was beginning to test his patience. Jacob kept casting nervous glances over at Jana. She still looked pale, slumped in a chair and only half paying attention.

“Fine. I’ll tell you. But swear on your mother that you’ll hand me over to the Lebanese authorities.”

“Fine. I swear on my mother.”

“You too,” the smuggler told Jana.

“Huh?”

Damn. She’s fading fast.

“I said swear on your mother that you’ll hand me over to the Lebanese authorities.”

“I swear.”

He turned to Hervé Boucher.

“I was raised in an orphanage,” the Frenchman told him. He fished out a gold cross on a chain tucked beneath his shirt. “I am a practicing Catholic. I’ll swear on Jesus Christ.”

With that, he kissed the cross and put it back beneath his shirt.

“Fine. General al-Rashid is planning to develop bioweapons, just like you thought. That’s why he raided those disease centers.”

“Why so far apart? Getting the ones in Iraq and Kurdistan would have been a lot harder than hitting, say, Turkey.”

“He wanted samples of certain diseases stored at those places rather than ones that would be easier to hit. I don’t know the details.”

“And your shipment to him included unlisted equipment for reproducing those diseases.”

“Yes. There were several boxes falsely labeled that had devices and chemicals not on the manifest.”

“For cultivating bacteria or viruses? Or both?”

“I don’t know. I don’t even know the full contents of those boxes. A lot of technical names in German I wasn’t familiar with.”

“German?” Jana sounded confused.

“The order came from a German pharmaceutical company,” Boucher said, his brow furrowing a bit in confusion. That had been in the intel. They had discussed it.

Jacob looked at his girlfriend with renewed worry.

Ibn Omar went on. "The shipment will have reached him by now, and he will have had plenty of time to set up the laboratory. The general has recruited top scientists from Syria and Iraq, visionaries like himself who want an end to all this constant infighting. They already knew what to do with the samples once they got them, so by now they'll have created the diseases they plan to unleash on the world." The smuggler chuckled. "So you see, you're already too late."

"Those diseases will kill Arabs too," Jacob said.

"They'll be spread in the West through General al-Rashid's agents. Of course, they will spread globally and eventually return to this region, but by then the general's scientists will have developed vaccines that he will give free to every Arab, regardless of their loyalties. This will turn the people's hearts to our great cause."

"And where did he get the money for all this?" Jacob asked. He already knew part of the answer. He wanted to see if the smuggler would be honest.

"Some oil baron in Dubai. I didn't recognize the name and I think the name is fake. Whoever he is, he is a very rich man and a visionary like the general."

Jacob hesitated, then said, "Have you ever heard of The Order?"

"The what?"

The man's confusion seemed genuine.

"Is the general working with any group besides this funder from Dubai?"

"No. Everyone's against him. That donation came as a surprise." Ibn Omar hesitated. "Wait, is this about the prisoner?"

Jacob felt his skin tingle. Jana perked up.

"What prisoner?" she asked.

"A Westerner they captured a couple of weeks ago. CIA or MI6. I don't know. I heard two of the general's soldiers joking about capturing him."

Jana leapt to her feet, stumbled, and grabbed the front of Ibn Omar's short. "Did you see him? What's his name? What are they doing to him?"

"I-I don't know. All I know is that they captured a Westerner. A spy, they said. I don't know anything more. The general is keeping him close by. He thinks he's valuable."

"Tell us!"

"I don't know anything more. I'm in the import/export business. It's not my job to know about prisoners. I don't want to know."

Jacob let out a frustrated sigh. What the man said made sense. Why would he want to know these things? It could put him in danger.

But they were one step closer to Aaron …

"So where are these laboratories?" Jacob asked. "I presume the address on the manifest wasn't the final destination?"

"No."

"So … "

The smuggler gave him a defiant look. "Why should I tell you?"

"Because you haven't given us any valuable intel yet. You're mostly telling us what we already know. That's pissing me off. And if you keep pissing me off, you're going to the Andes for the rest of your life. No goodbye to family, no chance to ever see them again. You vanish like a ghost, and a ghost will all you'll be."

Ibn Omar grimaced and looked around him as if hoping to see some sign of reassurance or a means of escape. After a moment, he looked back at Jacob.

"Tel al-Gazal."

"What's that?" Jacob knew that a "Tel" was an ancient mound which built up over centuries of habitation. "Gazal" meant gazelle, so probably only a placename. Obviously some archaeological site.

"I've heard of it," Jana said. "It's an Assyrian site in northeastern Syrian near the Iraqi border."

Jacob's heart lifted a little. Nothing like archaeology to get Jana going again.

"The general is a great lover of history," Ibn Omar said. "He saved many antiquities from ISIS when they were destroying them as un-Islamic. While the general is firm in his religion, he is not a radical, and he sees no threat from the ancient things. Instead, he sees them as proof of the greatness of the Arab people."

Jacob knew enough history to know that this region didn't have any Arabs in it until the great expansion out of the Saudi peninsula in the 7th and 8th centuries, the first great conquests of Islam. The Assyrian civilization flourished way before that. He decided not to correct him. At last, the guy was giving some intel they could use.

The smuggler went on.

"He has many bases around his territory, and of course spends much of his time on the front line, but his main base, and where he has put the laboratory, is at Tel al-Gazal. It was a fort in Assyrian times. The general has always looked up to the Assyrians as the greatest warriors in the ancient Middle East."

That was true. Jacob remembered Jana showing him around the British Museum, pointing out the huge stone bas-reliefs taken from some Assyrian palace. They depicted battles and sieges where the Assyrians used sophisticated devices such as siege towers fitted with battering rams. In one scene, the army was crossing a river using inflatable animal skins as flotation devices while archers on the riverbank covered their advance.

They were cruel to their enemies, too, cutting off hands and heads. Jana told him one account where they had ordered a city to submit. When the defenders showed defiance, the Assyrians laid siege to the city, took it, and covered the city walls with the skins of all the men. The women and children they led into slavery.

If that was the culture General al-Rashid idolized, then they had yet another reason to stop him.

“When does he plan to release the contagion, and what countries is he going to target?”

“I don’t know. I didn’t need to know, so I was not told. All I know is that he plans to release several diseases in several countries at once."

“What else can you tell us about his base at Tel al-Gazal?”

“I’ve never been there. I just know he has his command center there and the labs. I am sure it is well guarded. They’ll cut you down if you step within a kilometer of the place.”

Jacob grinned. “Don’t be so sure.” He turned to Boucher. “I presume you have a secure computer and a satellite uplink in this place?”

“Of course.”

“Let’s get to work.”

They moved into another room that acted as the Frenchman’s home office. Jana wobbled after them.

Jacob put a hand on her shoulder. “Why don’t you lie down?”

“I’m fine.”

“You are not fine,” he said gently. “We can handle this. We’ll share with you everything we find out and you can go over it, *after* you take a nap.”

Jana nodded and shuffled off to the bedroom. Jacob looked after her, worry aching his heart.

CHAPTER EIGHTEEN

"This sure looks like a base," Jacob said, examining the satellite imagery of Tel al-Gazal and the surrounding area as he sat next to Hervé Boucher.

The ancient site, visible as a low mound of earth cut with faint traces of foundations, stood near two villages, two of many that dotted a region where farmers scraped out a living with limited water and depended as much on their herds of sheep and goats as they did on their crops. A paved road ran through the bigger one, but they were well away from any major center of population.

The villages stood near the Iraqi border, close to the smuggling and trade routes that brought the Syrian People's Front much of their income. The spot was about halfway between two battlefronts, one against the Islamist al-Nusra, and the other against Assad's forces.

Not a bad place to put a command post.

Jacob was even more convinced by the closeup images. While the French and the CIA hadn't taken many shots of this area, not realizing its importance and not being overly concerned by the Syrian People's Front until now, they did have good images from every other week stretching back several months.

And they showed a lot of changes.

Six months ago, there was a small base here, a crude fort made of concrete walls with a couple of buildings inside that couldn't have housed more than thirty guys. More of an outpost, probably only to keep an eye on this border region and the local population. Nothing special. Then, five months ago, the operation had doubled in size.

They had tried to hide it. The new buildings were scattered across both villages with an outpost on the road, but it was obvious they had doubled their local garrison.

Then, four months ago, two large buildings were constructed very quickly. The significant detail was they were not built next to the original base or the road, so they didn't appear to have either a military or a commercial purpose. The speed with which they were built in this marginal region showed that the Syrian People's Front considered their construction important.

A close study to the satellite imagery didn't reveal their purpose. Each was twice the size of the largest house, rectangular and of one story. Both were supplied with extra electricity and sizeable backup generators.

Once the roofs were on, there was a flurry of activity, with trucks coming and going and a large shipment just about the time the "medical" supplies should have arrived.

Then, a month ago, a large cluster of tents appeared next to the two new buildings, capable of housing perhaps a hundred people. The resolution was good enough to show many of these newcomers didn't wear khaki or olive drab, but white.

Lab coats?

"I'm convinced," Jacob said, turning to the French agent. "What about you?"

"I'll call my people and you call yours. Have you checked on Jana?"

"I'll let her sleep a bit more."

Boucher nodded, looking as worried as Jacob felt.

Jacob got on his satellite phone and called Tyler Wallace. The old soldier answered on the second ring.

"How are you, Agent Snow?"

"Good. I have a lot to tell you."

"Where's Agent Peters?"

"Resting."

"Is she all right?"

Jacob hesitated. "Exhausted."

"That's it?"

Jacob smiled. You couldn't slip much by that man.

"Her head's hurting. She took a bump to that injury from the last mission."

Wallace's brow furrowed with concern. "She should have it looked at."

"Let me tell you what's going on first."

Jacob related everything they had experienced and learned so far. Tyler listened with intense concentration, occasionally asking a question but otherwise not interrupting. When Jacob finished, Tyler nodded.

"It sounds like you have a good lead on both Aaron Peters and the bioweapons. I'll talk with the director and our associates in Paris and see if we can get you some backup for the raid."

“Sir, we need to get there now. We can’t perform an airstrike because that might release the contagion. The base is near two centers of population. We have to have boots on the ground.”

“I understand that, but there are only three of you. You’re going to need backup, especially since Agent Peters is injured. You’re not at one hundred percent either.”

“All right. How long?”

“Hard to say. The French probably have troops close to the area. Of course we do too, but getting permission for a raid on a faction that’s never attacked us is going to be tricky.”

“Sir, they’re an imminent threat.”

“I’m aware of that, and I value your intel. You two always come up with the answers. I’m just saying that the president probably will hesitate to authorize a raid. If it’s led by the French, it will be easier.”

Then I sure hope Hervé convinces his boss.

“Any news on Aaron? Anything to confirm he’s the man they have prisoner?” Jacob asked.

“I’m afraid not. We’re pursuing several leads.”

“Leads?”

“That’s all we have at the moment, Agent Snow.”

“Jana isn’t going to be happy about that.”

“I’m sorry. Looks like you’ve found out more than we have. We’re doing the best we can.”

“*You’re* doing the best you can.”

Tyler's face turned grim, and he gave a curt nod. He knew what Jacob meant.

The Order might still have moles within the CIA. They might be dragging their feet in the investigation or deliberately misleading it. Tyler knew this, and also knew he didn't have time to do everything himself. At some point, he had to trust agents he couldn’t be one hundred percent sure of.

Tyler spoke.

“Have you found any evidence of … other involvements?”

“No. Of course, we haven’t had much contact with the enemy, just that sniper and this smuggler. Both are local agents and work on a need-to-know basis.”

“I see. Get some rest. We’ll get on this as quick as we can.”

“Thank you, sir.”

“I’ll be in touch soon.”

Jacob nodded and hung up. He went back to the living room to find a crestfallen Salim ibn Omar exactly where they had left him. Jacob checked his bonds and patted him playfully on the shoulder.

"Cheer up. At least you're not going to the Andes."

A moment later, Boucher came out of the other bedroom.

"What's the news, Hervé?"

Boucher glanced at the smuggler and led Jacob into the kitchen, where he closed the door and began to prepare some coffee.

"I spoke with the chief of the General Directorate of External Security and he agrees with our assessment. He's going to speak with the president and prime minister. There's a French base in Syria that has a strike force. They're French Foreign Legion and have done raids like this before."

"When can they be ready to move out?"

"When they get authorization," he grumbled, grinding the coffee beans with more force than necessary. "Until then, we're supposed to stay here."

"We have an expression in the American army. 'Hurry up and wait.'"

Boucher nodded. "Yes. We have a similar expression. I hope they don't keep us waiting long, because I have the feeling that we don't have much time."

***

Authorization didn't come for another five hours, by which time night had fallen and they had eaten dinner. Jana had slept three hours and still looked weary. Boucher sat them down to a three-course meal of remarkable quality, considering everything came out of a can.

The DGSE replied first, authorizing a strike force of the French Foreign Legion to fly from northern Syria, where they were engaged in training the Kurds, to take out the biowarfare labs at Tel el-Gazal. Given that it would be a French-led operation, that gave the Americans more confidence to authorize their two agents to go along. Not having soldiers in the line of fire made it easier politically. Jacob knew that if he or Jana got killed, there wouldn't be any reports of it to the press. They would simply vanish.

No medals. No statue. No memorials in the newspaper. That was the nature of this business. You did it because you had to, because the world needed you to.

Other than a couple of necessary trips to the bathroom, Salim ibn Omar had remained tied to the chair in the living room. They spoon-fed him a bit of dinner and then went back into the kitchen to discuss plans.

"A colleague will come here and take care of the apartment and ibn Omar," Boucher told them. "Then we will go to the airport where a private plane will take us first to Turkey, and then to the base in northern Syria."

"We need to get Jana to a hospital to have her head looked at," Jacob said.

Boucher looked about to agree when Jana cut him off.

"We don't have time for that."

"But—"

"We barely have time to get where we need to go and hit the base at dawn. We can't afford to wait another day. It has to be tomorrow. I'll rest on the plane, and maybe someone in the French base can have a look at me. I'll hang back in the raid, too, but we need to go now."

Jacob wanted to object, and yet knew she was right. He put a hand on her shoulder.

"Fine, but you rest the whole way. Boucher and I and the regimental commander will take care of all the planning. You'll be on the raid as a consultant in case we find something that requires your expertise."

"It's a deal." Jana gave him a weak smile. "I've always wanted to see Tel al-Gazal anyway."

"I'll call ahead to the legion," Boucher said, "and tell them to be ready to strike at dawn."

CHAPTER NINETEEN

Jacob really didn't want to fight a battle wearing a biowarfare mask, but he sure as hell didn't want to catch bubonic plague or SARS or whatever these idiots were cooking up.

They had flown to a private airstrip in Turkey before switching planes and flying into a portion of northern Syria held by the Kurds, an ethnic group who lived in Turkey, Iraq, and Syria and who had been oppressed by the governments of all three nations. Since the Iraq War and the fall of Saddam Hussein, the Kurds had retaken their traditional homeland in northern Iraq, using Erbil as their capital. Kurdistan was considered an autonomous province by the government in Baghdad, a myth everyone pretended to go along with so as to avoid another war. In reality, there was a border with different flags on either side, guarded by soldiers in different uniforms.

As far as Jacob was concerned, that meant they were two different countries.

The Kurds in Turkey had fought a long and unsuccessful campaign for independence, and now many had fled to Iraqi Kurdistan.

Others had fled to the Kurdish enclaves in Syria, where they fought for a local homeland.

The Kurds were always happy to help anyone fight those who fought them, and so gave the French Foreign Legion choppers permission to take off from their territory as long as the French didn't say they had ever been there.

So now they buzzed low over the desert to avoid the radar of whoever might be watching, the first hint of dawn turning the eastern sky a deep blue. They'd land two miles east of the target and quick march there, hitting the base before dawn or perhaps in the first light of dawn when the rising sun would dazzle the defenders' eyes.

It all depended on how fast they could get there.

He rode in one of three Airbus NH90 helicopters, each carrying 20 French Foreign Legionnaires. They were heavily armed with assault rifles, a couple of machine guns, and several RPGs. They also wore Kevlar and biohazard masks.

Jacob worried they were too heavily equipped and that the weight would slow them down in the assault.

But that hadn't been his call, and he couldn't really blame the commander, a grizzled colonel who had been shaken out of bed and given an assignment at the last minute. He wanted to protect his men, who had to go against a force of unknown size with no air cover and the possibility of bioagents being deployed on the battlefield.

Jacob thought he already knew all the French swear words, but Colonel Roux taught him several more.

He glanced over at Jana, who was as geared up as the rest of them. She swore she was ready for battle, but caved quickly when Jacob suggested she hang back with the rearguard and the medics.

Still, Jacob felt guilty about bringing her along. He was the senior agent and could technically order her to stay in Turkey, but she wouldn't have stood for it. Not when this raid provided the best chance of finding her father.

Despite the tension, Jacob smiled. He could stand up to anyone in the world other than his girlfriend. He would have gotten into a boxing ring with Chingis before doing that.

It bothered him that they hadn't found any solid evidence of involvement by Dr. Harlow or The Order. Salim ibn Omar hadn't heard of General al-Rashid getting any outside help except for that mysterious donor.

That must be the connection. The Order had funded several disruptive organizations before in order to further their own mysterious ends.

Yeah, this plan had their fingerprints all over it.

The helicopter touched down, the door slid open, and Colonel Roux shouted at his men to get out.

The legionnaires swarmed out of the chopper, wearing night vision goggles to see through the last few minutes of darkness. By the time Jacob got out, halfway back in line, the other two choppers had landed and men had taken up position all around the perimeter, barely visible as vague shapes in the swirl of sand lifted up by the rotor blades.

Hunkering low, Jacob followed the main body moving west. He was grateful for the night vision goggles and biohazard mask stopping all that manmade sandstorm from overwhelming him, but he worried about its effect on the troops in the quick desert march ahead.

After fifteen minutes, his worries came true. The men started panting and sweating despite the chilly desert predawn air. With a few choice swear words, Colonel Roux ordered everyone to take off their masks.

"We'll put them back on when we make contact," he ordered.

"He could have made that decision fifteen minutes ago," Hervé Boucher said, stripping off his mask.

"What was that?" the colonel snapped.

"I said good decision, sir!"

Jacob grinned. He wouldn't want to go up against that officer, not even with a razor blade hidden in his belt buckle.

He wouldn't want to go up against any of these guys, all hulking men from rough neighborhoods or port cities like Marseilles, the unwanted of France who had gone overseas to forge a new bond and make a new life taking on the toughest assignments their country could give them. He had fought by the side of the French Foreign Legion before, and he knew they could do the job.

The column jogged through the desert, an eerie green landscape through their night vision goggles. The desert here was flat and gritty with few dunes and only scrubs and the occasional palm tree for vegetation. A glance over his shoulder to check how Jana was doing only showed him a bright glow. The horizon was getting brighter and warmer. Soon, the sun would rise.

They might not make it in time.

Colonel Roux must have worried about the same thing, because he ordered the men to go faster.

God, I hope Jana can keep up.

Jacob focused forward. He could see the first of the buildings in the distance.

They cut left to where recon had already told them was a wadi with steep sides about eight feet deep. Two advance scouts had already secured the dry riverbed, which would get them closer to the terrorist base without being seen.

Jacob and his comrades got in and jogged along the sandy bottom. He was surprised to see no bodies. The scouts didn't have to overpower any sentries. These guys were idiots for not securing such an obvious approach point.

Unless they mined it.

They didn't have time to scan it with metal detectors. The eastern sky was brightening enough that everyone took off their night vision goggles. They were useless encumbrances now.

When their GPS told them they were at the closest point to the base that the wadi would get them, they stopped and lined up on the edge. Colonel Roux and Jacob crawled up the side and scanned the area with their binoculars.

The eastern sky had turned from deep blue to salmon, giving enough natural light to see the village a bit to the left, with more houses off to the right. In the center stood the two new buildings and a concrete-walled compound next to it, between their position and the labs. The cluster of tents was barely visible just beyond. A few people moved around the villages, and they could see a couple of silhouettes atop the concrete wall.

Colonel Roux checked his watch, then turned to the men in the wadi.

"The sun will rise in exactly three minutes. Then we're going over the top."

The men spread out along the wadi so that when they charged, they would make less of a target. Each man put on their biohazard mask. They did not need to be told.

Jacob dropped down and went over to Jana, who sat on the wadi's sandy bottom, panting. He sat down next to her and put a reassuring arm around her shoulders.

"Are you OK?"

"My head hurts and I'm more tired than I should be. At least we're almost done."

She put on her mask with obvious reluctance.

Jacob gave her shoulder a squeeze. He was not convinced they were almost done.

She is, though. After this, she's going to have to rest, whether we've completed the mission or not.

"After this we'll fly to Istanbul or Athens or somewhere and have you properly looked at."

The forward base of the French Foreign Legion had a combat medic who had examined her and confirmed complications arising from her recent concussion, but the base lacked the proper equipment to make a full diagnosis. Jana needed an MRI, not a quick checkup by a guy more accustomed to dealing with gunshot wounds.

Jacob put a hand on her shoulder and squeezed. Then he got back into position.

Hervé Boucher caught his eye and gave him a thumb's up. Jacob nodded in return.

They didn't have time to do more before the first rays of sun peeked over the horizon and bathed the top of the concrete compound in light.

Colonel Roux called out, "Let's wait a minute."

As the sun rose, more of the compound was lit, as was the village beyond it. First the top of the minaret, then the rooftops, and finally the entire buildings. The two figures atop the concrete fort hadn't moved. Jacob could just make out a small group of people standing among the tents. He thought they wore white, but they were too far off to tell.

"Charge!" Colonel Roux shouted in French. It was the same word in English, and men and women going into battle did it the same way, with a tight gut and laser focus.

They crested the wadi bank and pelted across the open space in front of the fort and village. Two men with shoulder-mounted rockets remained in the wadi and fired. The rockets streaked overhead, one hitting the parapet where the two sentries were posted and the other hitting another section of the upper wall.

Both explosions were powerful enough to tear off big chunks of concrete, sending them flying in all directions. Hopefully, several terrorists inside the fort would get hit. Anyone on the catwalk was already dead.

Jacob kept running, keeping in line with the legionnaires. No return fire came. Other than a few screams and the villagers running away, they saw no sign of movement.

Are we charging into an ambush?

They kept running, every eye scanning for movement or return fire.

There was nothing.

As the smoke cleared from atop the fort, they saw the crumbled remains of the wall totally unoccupied. Two more French rockets slammed into the wall, punching through and sending deadly fragments into the interior.

A couple of men at the center of the line went prone, snipers ready to take out anyone who showed themselves. But no one showed themselves. The rest of the line peeled off into two halves, moving to either side of the fort and keeping a close eye on it. Another two rockets slammed into the weak concrete, blowing another pair of holes into it.

Shoddy workmanship. Wouldn't stop more than small arms fire or the weaker RPGs, Jacob thought. *You can barely call it a fort at all.*

That made him wonder.

He wondered even more when he got to the side of the fort and saw the gate open. There was nothing inside except a couple of small buildings, one now in flames thanks to the rockets.

No vehicles. No people. Nothing.

Some men peeled off to check out the interior, sending up a flare to tell the rocket guys to hold off, although that was just a precaution since they must have seen their current position. The rest of the line continued toward the tents and the two laboratory buildings.

That cluster of men still stood among the tents. They hadn't moved.

And they still weren't moving. At all.

They didn't have to go much further to see they were all mannequins.

Some were dressed in khaki or olive drab, others in lab coats.

They've been moving them around to fool the spy satellite, the tricky bastards.

No fire came from the village. Some of the legionnaires kept the village under cover while the rest passed through the tents. It was obvious from their movements that they weren't finding anything.

Jacob ended up with the part of the team that hit the nearest lab building. One man lobbed a grenade at the front door, and everybody took cover.

It detonated, setting off a bigger explosion. The door had been booby-trapped. A double explosion over at the other building told them that the other team had uncovered an identical trap.

When the smoke cleared, they saw the building was an empty shell.

They had been fooled. There was no biowarfare lab here. They hadn't even seen any evidence of fighters. Those silhouettes on the fort's parapet hadn't moved before getting blown apart. They were probably dummies, just like the ones standing around the tents.

We're the real dummies here. Now, we have no idea where to look.

CHAPTER TWENTY

General Tariq al-Rashid put away his phone and turned to his second-in-command, the Bedouin Qa'dan al-Nimir.

"They hit the base at Tel al-Gazal," the general said.

The Bedouin laughed. "Stupid Westerners. I knew they'd fall for it!"

The general smiled, but did not laugh. "They will continue their search. It won't be long until they find this place."

"The scientists say they are almost ready."

"What do they mean by 'almost'?"

The Bedouin snorted. "Who knows with those weak bookworms? Let's go ask, and put the fear of Allah's wrath into them if they do not meet their deadline."

They headed out of the general's office and down the main street of the village of Al Atlal. A football match was going on in a space between two houses. Some of the local boys were squealing with excitement and kicking a battered old ball. The goalie for one team pointed out the two men, and the boys turned to look. The general recognized Asif.

"Come watch us!" the boy called over. "You said you'd watch and say who's best."

"Sorry, we have urgent business."

The boys ran over.

"Another attack?" Asif asked, at the forefront of the boys as usual.

"Yes."

"Will there be tanks?"

The boys looked at him eagerly. The general smiled. Qa'dan al-Nimir, despite his dour demeanor and his lack of patience with interruptions, smiled too. That smile held a note of sadness. He had lost two sons about the age of these boys to that Coalition airstrike.

"No, it's a different attack this time."

"Tell us! Tell us!"

The general brought a finger to his lips. "It's a secret. Soon you will know, but as future soldiers I want you all to swear you will tell nothing of this attack until you hear about it on the radio."

The boys nodded solemnly.

"We promise, general," Asif said, speaking for all.

The two men headed out, then stopped after a few paces when the boys followed.

"We're not going to the Tel this time, young soldiers," General al-Rashid told them. "We have some secret business."

"You can trust us!" Asif said.

The general smiled. "Maybe next time. Enjoy your game."

The two men walked on alone, passing by the Tel on their way to the lab in the outlying village. The general cast an appreciative eye over the ancient site. He'd love to conduct an excavation there someday. It had always been his dream to be an archaeologist, but he had grown up poor in Assad's Syria. Such dreams were only for Westerners or rich Arabs. His only choices for advancement were to try and rise up the ranks of the military or become a bandit. He was too honorable to be a bandit, so he joined the army, only to find it lacking in honor as well.

Once all this is done, perhaps I will hire a team of archaeologist to excavate this place and Tel al-Gazal. I hope those Westerners didn't damage it during their raid.

The Westerners ...

How much time do we have?

Without realizing it, General al-Rashid quickened his pace.

They got to the lab, which on the outside looked like a series of houses clustered together but which actually had doorways in the connecting walls to make one larger building.

A few men were milling around, taking care of flocks of goats and sheep, or tilling small gardens set near the houses. Others, dressed as women, sullenly went about the women's work of drawing water and cooking.

"All for the greater cause, my friends," the general called to them. "All for the greater cause."

A few managed a smile.

He chuckled. These were hardened veterans. To submit them to such humiliation was unfair, even if they understood its importance. He had increased the pay of the "women" in this village and boasted how he was even more progressive than the West, because didn't women there always complain they got paid less?

The "women" didn't laugh at the joke, although they took the extra pay eagerly enough.

General al-Rashid glanced up at the clear blue morning sky. Was a satellite staring down at them right now? Hard to say. This was just one of many bases, no bigger than most and smaller than some. There was no reason for the Americans or the Jews to notice it. His plan was safe for the moment.

Perhaps. It was a bad strategy to underestimate the enemy.

They came to a door of a regular-looking house, where they knocked. A slit opened in the door, the man behind it recognized his superior officers, and he immediately slid back the bolt and opened.

General al-Rashid and his second-in-command stepped out of a village street and into what should have been a humble dwelling but was in fact the most advanced biological laboratory in the country, all funded by that generous and mysterious donor from the Gulf.

They stopped at an inner door, where they had to put on hazmat suits. Then, they had to step into a shallow tray full of some sort of liquid and get sprayed by one of the technicians. General al-Rashid wasn't sure what all this was for, but he knew that a good leader always trusts the specialists on his team.

He and his second-in-command then passed through a second door and entered a large, brightly lit room full of computers. Several men and even a few women, all dressed in hazmat suits, were hard at work here. While he had been reluctant to hire women, there was a shortage of willing specialists in the region and they had turned out to be excellent workers. He had made his own female cousin an officer and put her in charge of their safety. Most of his men wouldn't listen to a woman's commands, but his cousin spoke with his voice.

They passed through a doorway into what looked like from the outside to be another house. Here, they came to the actual lab. A few of the senior staff were studying cultures under microscopes while a large freezer hummed to one side.

One of the women looked up. Dr. Aisha Yasin, formerly of the University of Damascus until her husband was arrested, tortured, and killed for being a dissident and she had to flee with her children to rebel-held areas to escape a similar fate. His operative found this leading microbiologist working as a nurse for the Red Cross at a refugee camp on the Turkish border and made an offer that had stoked up the fires of vengeance in her heart.

"Good morning, General," she said, standing at attention and snapping out as much of a salute as her hazmat suit would allow. Dr. Yasin thought of herself as part of the military wing of the Syrian

People's Front. A silly notion, but if it made her do her job better, he did not object.

"Good morning, Dr. Yasin. How is the cultivation coming along?"

She stood a little straighter and behind the plastic face mask, her middle-aged face cracked into a rare smile. "General, I am proud to report that we have successfully recreated all the cultures. We are just finalizing the last of the production units. Allow me to show you."

The general nodded. "I would be most interested."

The microbiologist led them to another door leading to another "house." They passed through to a similar room to the one they had just left. Here a large freezer was being stocked by one of the senior researchers. When the figure turned in his awkward suit, the general recognized Dr. Mohammed Abadi. An older man who had returned from a safe and comfortable job in Europe to join the fight, he did not salute. He merely bowed his head and touched his hand to his heart as a sign of respect. The man was thirty years his senior, so the general allowed this. He had always respected his elders, especially elders as useful as this one.

Dr. Abadi walked over to a desk and picked up what looked like an ereader.

"We have perfected the delivery package, sir. We have taken a standard model ereader and hollowed it out, leaving only enough room for this little light on the bottom to shine red if someone attempts to turn on the device. As you can see, the screen is blank. If anyone checks the device at customs, our delivery men can claim it is out of power after using it on a long flight. But look at this."

He slid it open to reveal a flat culture dish inside.

Qa'dan al-Nimir took a step back. Dr. Abadi laughed, a dangerous thing to do with the Bedouin.

"Do not fear. This culture dish is empty, and even if it was full, we have produced dishes that are hermetically sealed. You wouldn't even need your hazmat suit to protect you."

"Interesting," General al-Rashid said before his second-in-command could snap at the scientist. "But won't the culture go bad if it's not kept in freezing conditions?"

Dr. Yasin cut in. "It will slowly thaw, but as it does it will become live. The bacteria inside, and the virus for the other sample, will both survive for twenty-four hours, plenty of time to get to the target city. After that, all the operative needs to do is open this false ereader, then open the culture dish in a public place. The contagion will be released, contagions that haven't been seen in centuries, millennia even!"

Even wearing hazmat suits, the general could see the excitement in the two scientists' posture.

"It is a remarkable achievement," he said. "You and your team will go down in history as great warriors for the Arab people."

Both microbiologists murmured their appreciation.

"We have more good news, general," Dr. Yasin said. "We have completed the cultures and tested the most potent one on the test subject."

"Excellent! Let's go see how the unbeliever is doing, shall we?"

"Right this way, general."

The two head scientists led them to a back room, where a steel door with a window of bulletproof glass looked in on a tiny cell.

A man was strapped to a chair there. This was a Russian spy they had caught in their territory, no doubt gathering intelligence for Assad's forces. It was a major coup to grab him, and the men had boasted about it to everyone who visited. They had tortured him for information and were about to execute him when the scientists requested him as a lab rat.

When the general looked through the window, he saw that executing him would have been a mercy.

The man's eyes were feverish, his skin covered with suppurating boils. His hair had come off in patches, and what had once been a powerful body had thinned and shook with fever and was wracked by a persistent cough.

"We infected him less than twenty-four hours ago and he should be dead within a few hours," Dr. Yasin said. "Sensors inside the room show that his coughing has led to a high density of the virus in the air. He is extremely contagious, just like we hoped."

"Excellent work! Soon, millions of Westerners will be feeling the same."

"Yes," she replied, beaming with pride. "Now we only have to check that each is properly cultivated and fully frozen, then fit each into one of these ereaders."

"And when will our operatives get them?" the general asked.

He had ten operatives ready with passports to various EU countries as well as three with American passports. They were all ready and waiting to get smuggled across the border to Turkey, an easy enough task, and then they would board flights in Ankara to take them to their destinations. The cultures on the American flights would come live while they were in the air, but that was all right. The passengers and crew would become carriers once they disembarked. The three men flying to America knew this and were willing to give their lives for their people.

"When will they get to leave?" Dr. Yasin smiled. "This afternoon, general. Our plans will begin to bear fruit by tomorrow."

"Tomorrow … " General Tariq al-Rashid whispered. "By tomorrow, the sick societies of the West will be sick for real."

CHAPTER TWENTY ONE

While the legionnaires cleared the two villages and searched the empty buildings that had lured them here, Jana was hard at work on a computer with a satellite uplink.

She needed to find out where General al-Rashid's lab really was.

That was hard to narrow down. He controlled a large section of the country filled with countless villages, dozens of towns, and a couple of midsized cities. He could be anywhere.

Jacob and Boucher kept coming back to her with reports from the search. They had found no evidence that this place had been used for anything but a decoy. The villagers swore they knew nothing. The troops who had been stationed here had told them they were expanding the base. That was all.

They did find out that General Tariq al-Rashid had come to oversee the construction personally. Jana supposed that was an added layer of deception. Word would have spread that the famous leader had been doing some important work next to Tel al-Gazal. That would have made this place even more of a target.

It was only after Jacob returned the third time to report that he brought some useful information.

And he didn't even know he was doing it.

"Not finding a damn thing," he grumbled. "I did meet the head schoolteacher. He had a shed full of Assyrian artifacts from that Tel over there. Tons of stuff. You would have loved it. He said when the general was here, he captured some antiquities thieves digging at the site and sentenced them to forced labor. Then he confiscated all their loot and gave them to the schoolteacher. Gave him money to set up a museum too. The guy's already built the foundation behind his house. Al-Rashid said he wants all the schoolchildren to know about their heritage."

"Huh. That's weird."

"What? A Middle Eastern militant can't be interested in history? You're always complaining that I'm not interested enough."

"No, what's weird is that he wouldn't sell the artifacts himself. They're a major source of income for poor communities here. ISIS sold a bunch of artifacts even while they were smashing others."

"Salim ibn Omar told us that the general is a history buff. I guess he was telling the truth. Maybe that's why he set up next to this important archaeological site."

Jana snapped her fingers. "That's it!"

Jana had been staring at French and American spy satellite imagery. Now she got onto JSTOR, a database of academic publications, and found a map of archaeological sites in Syria. There were so many dots that they practically colored the entire country. An embarrassment of riches. She found another map that only showed Assyrian sites, then overlaid that on a map of General al-Rashid's territory.

"Bingo," she whispered.

There were a couple of dozen sites, but only five major ones, of which the one they were at was the largest.

She began to study the satellite imagery for all those sites.

It didn't take long to find two where there had been unusual activity in the past six months.

One was at Tel Hafa, named because the ancient site stood on a prominent ridge, "hafa" being the word for ridge in Arabic. It stood within sight of the Iraqi border and as such, was an important strategic location.

In the past few months, a fort standing near the site on the same ridge had been expanded, and a smaller fort had been built on the same ridge a couple of miles to the northwest. Both forts had new buildings inside them. Could this be the spot?

The other site was in the middle of nowhere, fairly close to the border with al-Nusra's territory and the scene of a recent offensive. Here there was a smaller Assyrian site next to a village called Al Atlal. A second village a kilometer away, too small to even be named on the map, had seen a bit of a building boom when a cluster of houses had been built in the past few months, increasing the number of buildings there by a third. The village of Al Atlal itself had received a new power plant that smudged some of the satellite images thanks to the unfiltered oil smoke it belched into the air.

When Jacob came back a fourth time, again with nothing new to report, she pointed to the two sites.

"I think it's one of these. General al-Rashid is an admirer of the Assyrians, and both of these places have Assyrian sites with a lot of recent construction nearby."

Jacob stared at the screen, flipping back and forth between the two sets of images.

"This one near the Iraqi border is in the perfect location to tap into the smuggling routes. That's probably why it's there in the first place."

"Yeah. That would have been useful to get the disease cultures from Iraqi Kurdistan, but I'm thinking that's not necessary since they obviously have a good enough smuggling network to get them all the way from Amman."

Jacob nodded. "Good point. This Al Atlal place is in the middle of nowhere, though."

"Maybe the general sees that as an advantage."

Jacob rubbed his jaw. "Yeah, maybe. Wait, go back to those images."

She flipped through the images of Al Atlal. When she went from an image six months ago to one taken five months ago, Jacob stopped her.

"What's that? What's going on there?"

"It's when the power plant came online."

"Yeah, just before the other village started to build those new houses. But there's no line going from Al Atlal to the smaller village."

"Maybe there is."

Jana zoomed in and together they studied the images, going back and forth, trying to see any anomalies.

They spotted it at the same time.

A thin black line running across the desert for a few yards. It ran in a line between the two villages.

"A power cable," Jacob said. "The sneaky bastards tried to cover it with sand but they hadn't covered it entirely when the spy satellite took this picture. They laid the extra power cable before they finished those houses, and they put the power station in Al Atlal to mask that they were really wiring electricity to this smaller village."

"We got it," Jana said.

"I think we do. Now we just need to convince the French."

"Convince them of what?" Boucher asked, coming into the room.

They explained everything they had discovered. Boucher gave a nod.

“I’ll make a call. The only problem is, the helicopters don’t have the range to get there with the current fuel. We’ll have to fly back to the base, refuel, and then go. That will take time.”

Time. Always, everything takes time. And what will General al-Rashid be doing in that time?

***

Boucher understood the time pressure perfectly well, and after convincing Colonel Roux to make a withdrawal to the helicopters, the intelligence operative made his call while they were enroute back to the Kurdish base.

The higher-ups in Paris conferred. Jana grew impatient while watching Boucher sit by his satellite phone, waiting for it to ring.

They waited. And waited. They landed, and the Kurds refueled their helicopters for an inflated price. Within an hour, they were ready to go. Now Colonel Roux joined Jana in staring at Boucher, who sat by the satellite phone placidly, chain-smoking.

“Can you hurry them up?” Jana asked.

“You don’t hurry these people,” Boucher replied.

Colonel Roux cursed under his breath.

Jana tried to relax. Her head had throbbed on that charge, but she had had some time to rest on the helicopter ride back. She felt all right at the moment, although tired.

The colonel decided not to waste time and studied the satellite imagery of the village of Al Atlal, zooming out to see the surrounding area and zooming in to see as much of the finer detail as he could.

Jana’s limited military training was sufficient to tell her this was a rough situation. The land was flat for miles around. There was no way to hide their approach or their assault. The weather wasn’t helping. Clean and calm. No dust clouds to reduce range of vision.

They’d have to go in hard and fast, and they’d have to do it in broad daylight with no convenient wadi to hide their approach. Another problem that was that they didn’t know how many troops they’d face. There was no fort here like in the other places, but there might be hidden fortifications, reinforced houses with firing slits. Snipers on the minarets of both mosques. Land mines.

What they could see were two Technicals, Jeeps with heavy machine guns mounted on the back. Mobile firepower made cheap. A popular item for any Third World militia.

But not the best general Tariq al-Rashid could muster. He had tanks. Russian-made Grad rocket launchers. Heavy artillery. Why didn't he have any of his more serious armaments guarding this village? Did he worry it would attract too much attention?

Or maybe they were hidden somehow.

Colonel Roux continued to educate them in creative French swear words. He made a call and came back, swearing even more.

"No possible reinforcements."

"How much air support can the helicopters give?" Jana asked.

"Minimal. They're transports, not fighters. They each have only a pair of missiles we don't dare use on any of the buildings in case we set off the contagion. They also have heavy machine guns we can use against any infantry, but that would bring them into range of any shoulder-mounted surface-to-air missiles or RPGs. Hell, even small arms fire can take down a chopper if there's enough of it. I don't want to risk the choppers when they're our only way out of there."

Jana sighed. This was looking like a bad move. Unfortunately, it was their only option to stop General al-Rashid.

It was also her only option to getting clues about Dad.

Just then, Boucher's satellite phone rang. He answered and spoke for a moment in low tones. Then he hung up and turned to them.

"We have approval. We move out now."

Jana took a deep breath and tried to control the pounding of her heart. She had a really bad feeling about this.

CHAPTER TWENTY TWO

For the second time in twenty-four hours, Jacob scrambled out of a helicopter with a unit of French Foreign Legionnaires. This time, they had touched down in an open field. The little village with the suspicious buildings stood not far off. In the distance they could see the Tel and beyond that, the village of Al Atlal.

Unlike last time, they could already see movement in the unnamed village. Distant figures were running around and twin plumes of dust told them those Technicals were on the way.

This was crazy. They had no knowledge of the enemy's strength and position, no real air support, and no secure line of withdrawal.

Hell with it. He'd been in worse fights.

They spread out in a line and charged the village. Once again, Jana joined the reserve line with the medics. She had looked tired on the trip over. Jacob tried not to worry about her. He had a more immediate problem right in front of him.

He could see men getting into position. Women too, throwing off their loose robes and headscarves and grabbing guns.

Fake women instead of dummies this time. And unlike the dummies, those fake women will fire back.

The flash of a gun from the top of the village's minaret. A legionnaire to Jacob's right grunted and fell, clutching his leg.

One of the men carrying a shoulder-mounted rocket launcher got to one knee and fired in a single fluid motion. The rocket sailed across the intervening distance, and the top of the minaret exploded.

Jacob gritted his teeth. He hated taking out religious structures. Why the hell did the militants insist on using them as sniper nests?

He knew why. Because minarets make perfect spots for snipers and if they got blown up, they made good propaganda on social media. To these scumbags, that was more important than preserving a house of worship.

They kept going. He couldn't see the cluster of new houses yet. They remained hidden behind some older structures. Fire came from the windows of a couple of the nearest buildings.

One of the legionnaires fired a rocket, and the small structure crumbled. Others poured fire on the second house, and the return fire stopped. Jacob prayed the civilians had gotten out in time. He'd seen them running, but had they all escaped?

This is why he preferred solo missions over military operations. In the military, things got real messy real quick.

Like what had happened to him in Afghanistan.

He tried not to think about that.

They passed the outmost houses, one now a smoking ruin, and into the village itself.

And then Jacob didn't have time to think about anything.

It became house-to-house combat, dirty and dangerous and with far more points of threat than one man could possibly watch.

Jacob knelt by a corner as a legionnaire stood over him. Jacob looked around the corner and fired just as an armed figure ducked into a doorway. The legionnaire fired too, but to the left, where someone had just shown himself at a window.

A cry told him the legionnaire had scored a hit. Jacob hadn't.

Just then, the legionnaire slammed into the stone wall of the hut and fell to the ground, a dent in his Kevlar.

Jacob searched desperately for who had fired and didn't see anyone. There was gunfire all around, and he could no longer pick out individual sounds.

Then, the shooter reappeared on a nearby roof. He aimed at someone behind Jacob, no doubt another Frenchman, but Jacob took him out before the Syrian could fire.

With a glance at the legionnaire, who seemed to have only had the wind knocked out of him, Jacob bolted for the doorway where the first guy had disappeared.

Just in time for a grenade to roll out of it.

Jacob kicked it back inside.

He wasn't quick enough. The grenade blew up inside, but before Jacob could dive for cover.

He felt a hot pain in his thigh and several impacts on his chest and helmet.

Like with his comrade, the Kevlar saved him.

Jacob flew back several feet and landed hard on his back.

For a moment, he lay there, ears ringing, trying to catch his breath. The gunfight swirled all around him, the rattle of small arms fire, the thud of grenade, the louder detonations of RPGs and the French missiles.

Then he heard a different sound—the sound of heavy machine guns.

The Technicals had appeared on the scene.

He rolled onto his stomach and saw one of them speed past an open space between two houses and disappear. He didn't see the other one at all.

His leg hurt. He checked and saw a shallow cut along the thigh. It was bleeding, but his leg still worked.

Good enough. He crawled a moment, found that to be painful but doable, and tried to get to his feet, leaning against the wall of the house for support.

No problem.

Well, it hurt, but no problem getting up. Jacob Snow was still in the game.

He took a quick look at his surroundings and saw that in the time that he had been down, which couldn't have been more than a minute, the battle had moved past him. Directly across from him, legionnaires were posted at both corners of a house firing at something beyond. At the house next to him, a legionnaire was just coming out, having cleared the building. He didn't see anyone else.

He heard them, though. There was the roar of a heavy machine gun, no doubt from that Technical he spotted, and the crackle of return fire. A grenade went off, but the Technical kept firing.

Jacob hurried to the nearest house corner, his leg jabbing with pain but functioning all right. He took a peek and saw the problem.

The Technical had parked itself in a walled garden or corral thirty yards away and a bit to Jacob's right. A chest-high stone fence protected everything except the gun itself, which had a large metal shield on the front to protect the gunner. Several legionnaires firing from nearby houses were having trouble hitting anything and had to spend most of their time with their heads down as the Syrian gunner poured fire on them. A couple of smoking craters showed where the French had tried throwing grenades at it, but they were too far away to get a decent throw without fully exposing themselves, and that would be suicide.

The gunner must have spotted Jacob, because he swung the machine gun around. Jacob ducked back. The corner of the stone house got chewed up by dozens of rounds before the gunner swung back to fire at someone else.

Where the hell were the French snipers? Or their guys with the rockets?

A boom in another part of the village told them where at least one of the rocket guys was. But they needed him here right now. Just before ducking back to avoid getting his head blown off, Jacob had seen figures advancing behind the Technical. It was going to act as covering fire for a counterattack.

Time to do something. Jacob had a couple of grenades, but he had the same problem as the legionnaires.

A Syrian appeared around the corner of another building and leveled his AK-47. Jacob took him out just as he fired, and the bullet hummed past Jacob's head.

Damn. This counterattack is only going to get worse. Everyone stationed at Al Atlal will be here in a minute.

Jacob chucked a grenade at the corner of that building to take out anyone coming up behind that guy, and then pelted across the little lane to the next row of houses, where a narrow alley between two houses that was at an angle he couldn't see into beckoned him with the promise of shelter. His leg wound protested with shrill pain. Jacob ignored it.

Running across the street like this was an amazingly stupid move that took the gunner in the Technical completely by surprise.

Firing three-round bursts as he went, Jacob saw his bullets smack off the armor plate or the stone wall as the gunner turned his machine gun in Jacob's direction.

Just as it came to bear, Jacob dove and tucked into a roll.

He heard the air rip apart just above him, dozens of heavy rounds barely missing him. The gunner stopped firing, adjusted, and Jacob kept rolling.

As he hoped, the legionnaires got emboldened by this distraction and poured fire at the Technical. Another grenade thudded.

But the Technical opened fire again. Bullets chewed up the ground all around Jacob, and for a harrowing second, he thought he wasn't going to make it, but then he rolled into the shelter of a narrow space between two houses.

He was safe, except he wasn't. Because as he leapt up, he saw the astonished face of a Syrian standing just in front of him, and the equally astonished face of the guy's buddy a few steps behind.

Jacob swung the butt of his assault rifle and caught the guy on the chin, then leveled it and fired a three-round burst into the belly of the man behind.

It turned out to be a two-round burst. He was out of ammo.

Good enough. The second man doubled over and fell to his knees.

A hit with the butt of his gun put him down and Jacob snapped in a new magazine, watching the other end of the alley, hoping no one would come around while he was defenseless.

Once he reloaded, the buzz of that heavy machine gun still filling the air, he moved to the far end of the alley. A child’s bicycle leaned against the wall. Jacob grimaced. He sure hoped their long approach had given all the civilians time to get out. Maybe this daylight attack was a good thing in that way.

He peeked around the corner where he knew that just beyond this house was the corral where the Technical was. The plan was to sneak up on its flank and toss a grenade.

That plan went to hell thanks to the half a dozen Syrians who sensed the threat he posed and were charging from the corral toward his position.

The lead one tossed a grenade.

A perfect throw. It landed right at the entrance to the alley.

Jacob kicked it back, nearly getting his foot shot off in the process, and followed it up with a grenade of his own.

When he next looked, he saw four of the six guys down and the other two staggering back, stunned.

Jacob took them out and moved forward. He didn't have any more grenades, and he didn't have time to search these bodies. He'd have to do this the hard way.

The hard way meant charging that mechanical monster while he could see reinforcements coming up in the distance. Some were on foot, sprinting the kilometer from Al Atlal. A plume of dust showed that some vehicles were coming from further off, probably sentries on the outskirts.

The Technical was still firing on the French. The gunner seemed unaware that he had been flanked. He probably assumed that all those guys going off to kill that one man who sprinted across the lane had taken care of the problem.

The gunner was still a good twenty yards away and partially covered by the side of the pickup truck. An easy shot.

Jacob aimed and fired.

The man jerked and fell.

A moment later, two more men showed themselves in the corral. One clambered up to take the gunner's place, and the other appeared with a light machine gun with a bipod. He braced the bipod on the stone wall and sent a burst in Jacob's direction.

Once again, Jacob had to squeeze against the stone wall of a villager's house to keep from getting blown apart. In the distance, he saw the reinforcements approaching across a dusty field. There was little cover between them and him other than a few shrubs. Soon they'd be in range and then he'd be a dead man. He already saw a couple of them get to one knee and fire long-range shots at him.

They missed, but they wouldn't miss for long.

And that Technical would start firing any moment.

CHAPTER TWENTY THREE

Jacob crouched at the corner of the stone building, unsure what to do. He couldn't stay put because the advancing Syrian reinforcements would soon get into close enough range to shoot him. He couldn't hit the Technical without getting gunned down by that guy with the light machine gun watching for him.

He could get into this house and try to fire from a window, but that would only buy him a bit of time. One of those guys was bound to toss a grenade inside.

He could retreat, but Jacob Snow was not accustomed to retreating.

Then, a miracle. There was a loud detonation from the direction of the Technical. Even around the corner, Jacob felt the shockwave.

The French had gotten one of their shoulder-fired rockets into action.

Jacob peeked around the corner and saw the corral was nothing but a smoking ruin backlit by flames from the vehicle. A bit further along, he saw a second column of oily smoke behind some houses. Was that the second Technical? With the firefight going on all around him, he hadn't heard that one go up.

The advancing reinforcements hesitated.

Then, one of the cars in the distance went up in flames. Beyond them, he could just make out one of the French helicopters sweeping through the air. Colonel Roux must have called in their one method of retreat as air support. The situation had gotten that desperate.

But now it looked like it was turning around as a second vehicle in the distance burst into a fireball.

There was still plenty to do. The cluster of new houses they had come here to investigate was just off to the left, if Jacob remembered right. It was easy to get turned around in this kind of fighting.

He angled to the left, as much to get some distance from those reinforcements as to get to the supposed lab, and met up with Colonel Roux and three of his men. The colonel's side was soaked with blood and he was swearing around a cigar, but he didn't look like he intended on slowing down.

Neither did Jacob. His leg burned like it had been doused in acid, but it still moved as good as the other one and he didn't feel faint from loss of blood. As long as his leg held him, he'd remain in the fight.

The cluster of new houses lay just ahead, a bit isolated from the rest of the village. As Jacob and the legionnaires approached, fire erupted from the corner of the new houses and the corner of an older house across the street.

Everyone flung themselves behind the shelter of a parked car, one of the few they'd seen in this little village. What was probably the prized possession of some local family got punctured with a dozen bullets, one of its tires deflating with an angry hiss.

Jacob and one of the Frenchmen popped up and fired. The two Syrians ducked back.

Then one of the Syrians reappeared with an RPG.

A hit with that would blow up the car and everyone near it.

Jacob and the legionnaire opened fire. Colonel Roux leapt out of cover to add his bullets.

The guy with the RPG went down.

Now that Colonel Roux was exposed, he didn't see any reason to hide himself again and charged full speed for the door to the suspected lab.

All right, I guess we're getting crazy now.

Jacob followed. The legionnaires didn't hesitate.

When the Syrian behind the suspected lab showed himself again, the sight of five guys charging them, one while smoking a cigar, made him decide not to get martyred that day and he ducked back behind the building. Jacob had a feeling they wouldn't be seeing him again anytime soon.

They got to the door. They put on their biohazard masks and the biggest legionnaire, who stood a full foot taller than Jacob and half again as wide, kicked the door.

Then he had to kick it again. Jacob didn't think anything short of a concrete wall could stand even one kick from this guy.

On the third kick, the door splintered and opened with a bang. They poured in and found themselves in a sort of antechamber with a rack of hazmat suits and a door on the far side. In front of the door was a tray filled with some sort of clear liquid. Everyone stopped.

"Merde," Colonel Roux whispered.

He turned to his men. “You guard this door and the door to the outside. Kill anyone who tries to enter or leave. The American and I will circle the building and check the windows.”

Jacob nodded. Going beyond that door looked like a really bad idea.

Then he noticed something. There had been a shuttered window right next to the door, but there was no sign of it on the inside.

Jacob went to the door, made sure the coast was clear, and glanced on the outside.

He was right. The window was a fake.

The colonel looked over his shoulder and saw the same thing. Just then, two more legionnaires came up. A shot rang out from the building where they had killed the guy with the RPG, which thankfully still lay in the street. They returned fire. The colonel ordered the two newcomers to stay put, and they rounded the building the way they had come. Every few paces, they came to a window and found them all to be fake.

"They did this to fool spy drones," the colonel said. "This building is a bunker, but they wanted it to look like a regular house."

Jacob nodded. They were good imitations. They even fooled the casual observer at ground level.

More legionnaires came up. Jacob spotted Jana in the distance giving first aid to a wounded Frenchman and he let out of breath of relief to see she was safe.

At least for the moment. While the fighting had died down a bit, this wasn’t over.

The colonel gave a few sharp orders, and the legionnaires moved out to secure the neighborhood. They couldn't leave the lab at the front line.

The advance began to gain pace. House to house. Tossing grenades to clear corners. Firing at anyone who showed themselves on rooftops or windows. The two French snipers had found good rooftop positions and took out several enemies before Jacob and the rest even saw them.

The Syrians, having lost both Technicals and having their reinforcements decimated by the helicopter, began to give ground. Jacob got the impression that their line was thinning, that those in the rear were peeling off and sneaking away. Only the hardcore remained.

The lab was now safely behind them. Jacob worried there might be a bomber inside the lab ready to set it off, but he thought the colonel’s caution was warranted. If they barged in there with only their masks, they might catch and spread the contagion they were trying to stop.

Jacob rounded a corner and saw a cluster of chicken coops and a wooden shed not far off. He thought he saw movement between the loose slats of the flimsy structure.

Something told him not to fire.

Then the shadows moved again, and he knew why. They were too short to be fighters.

Damn it. Kids are here!

He could hear shouting, too. A man in Arabic was shouting from behind the chicken coop. A high voice, too high to be an adult, replied. Jacob couldn't hear the words because of the ringing in his ears.

Jacob glanced around and saw no one. It was one of those eddies in a battle, a rare moment of stillness that was all too brief. Jacob advanced a bit, got in the cover of a doorway and waited.

He heard the crackle of a radio and the man speaking again.

"We can't fall back!" the young voice shouted.

"You're going back right now," the male voice replied. "All my troops are retreating."

"But General, you never retreat."

General!

"This is a tactical withdrawal. We've achieved our mission. Now we live to fight another day. Come. I need to get you out of here while there's still time. You should have never followed us here."

"We wanted to help!"

"No more arguing. Come."

Jacob pressed himself into the doorway to stay hidden. He heard footsteps. When he looked again, he saw General Tariq al-Rashid leading three boys aged about eleven to thirteen away from the battle. The general had an automatic rifle in his hand. Thankfully, the boys did not.

Damn it. I can't let him go.

But I can't risk the kids.

If you let him go, a lot of kids are going to die. And the contagion might come all the way back here and kill them, too.

Jacob hesitated a moment more, his heart torn.

I can't do it.

General al-Rashid took the boys to the entrance to a lane between the houses.

"Go! That's an order!"

The boys hesitated, then saluted.

"Go!"

They ran off.

General Tariq al-Rashid stood and watched them go. Then he gave a satisfied nod and turned back to the fighting.

Only to find Jacob standing out in the open a few yards away, a gun aimed at his head.

“Surrender now,” Jacob said.

The general grimaced. His gun was sloped, held only by one hand. There was no way he could bring it to bear before being torn apart by bullets.

“Drop it!” Jacob ordered.

He did not want to shoot this man, not after what he had just seen.

“If I do, will you promise not to go after the boys?”

“I don’t fight children.”

General al-Rashid sneered at him. "With all your bombings, you don't think you kill children? Well, at least you are acting honorably now."

He hesitated a moment longer, then threw his assault rifle on the ground.

“And the pistol,” Jacob ordered.

Carefully, General al-Rashid used two fingers to pull out the pistol in his holster and toss it on the ground next to the assault rifle.

He raised his hands in surrender. Jacob was dimly aware that the firing was beginning to die down. He kept his focus on the general.

General Tariq al-Rashid kept his hands up as he smiled.

"You're too late, Westerner. We have lost this battle, but we have already won the war."

CHAPTER TWENTY FOUR

Jana waddled in her hazmat suit behind a similarly suited team of French Foreign legionnaires. They had taken the suits from the antechamber of the laboratory complex. At her side was Gaston, a medic who specialized in biowarfare.

They kicked open the door, which was locked, and splashed through the tray of disinfectant liquid in front of it.

Beyond they found that the false houses were all connected into a series of computer rooms and labs. They met no resistance, only a team of hazmat-suited technicians who immediately put their hands up.

One stepped forward, bolder than the rest. Through the clear faceplate, Jana could see it was a middle-aged woman.

"I am Dr. Aisha Yasin of the University of Damascus," she said as the legionnaires spread out to secure all the rooms. "We will offer no resistance. We don't need to."

The woman's confidence worried her. Jacob had told her what the general had said when he had surrendered.

"General al-Rashid is our prisoner, as are many of your soldiers," Jana announced. "The rest have retreated beyond Al Atlal and are withdrawing into the desert. You've lost."

The woman slouched a little. "A pity, but they knew the risks. The important thing is that we win in the end."

"Have the cultures already been sent out?"

Dr. Yasin didn't respond.

Jana tried again. "Where are the cultures?"

"You'll get no cooperation from me or anyone on my team."

Jana pushed her aside and went to the largest computer desk in the room.

"I don't need to. Guys, cover them. Gaston, you're with me."

Jana sat at the computer and couldn't believe her luck. Not only was it on and didn't require a password, but it didn't appear to have had its hard drive wiped.

"They must have thought they would win," Gaston said in French with a chuckle.

Dr. Yasin cut in with the same language. "We already have won."

Jana turned to her. "Care to elaborate on that?"

No response.

"Hey!" one of the legionnaires called from another room. "They have a prisoner, and he looks European."

Jana was out of the chair like a shot. She ran to the other room, head throbbing, and saw the soldier looking through a thick window set in a steel door. Heart beating fast, Jana looked through.

She gasped. A man sat slumped in a chair, his skin covered with boils and bloody drool coming out of his mouth.

The man's features were so covered in boils and sores as to be barely recognizable, but he was definitely not her father. This man was shorter, and the hair color was wrong.

If it hadn't been for those two factors, she wouldn't have known.

"Who is that?" she demanded, going back into the lab.

"A prisoner. A test subject. There is nothing you can do for him. There is no cure for what he has, and he will be dead within the hour."

"Do you … have any more Western prisoners?"

"No," the female scientist said.

Jana grabbed her and dragged her to the cell.

"Tell me the truth or I'll rip off your hazmat suit and throw you in there with him!"

"It's true! We have no more prisoners. This is the first Westerner we've captured all year. You've taken over the village. You would have found more if there were more."

Jana slumped. This had all been a false lead. She wanted to sink to the floor in despair and not get up for days.

She took a deep breath, straightened her shoulders, and dragged Dr. Yasin back to the lab.

With a supreme effort of will, blinking away tears, she sat back down next to Gaston.

"Let's get to it," she mumbled.

Gaston plugged in an external hard drive.

"Let's go through the files before we start downloading anything," Jana said.

"Not yet. On this drive is a program that searches for deleted files. People think that deleting a file is enough, but they are still on the hard drive. There are programs to wipe files clean, but even those leave a trace. This program will find anything they have deleted. It's far more powerful than anything on the commercial market and unless they have a top-grade hacker in this lab, it will find anything they tried to wipe."

Gaston ran the program. It came up with more than a hundred files.

The Frenchman let out a low whistle. "They have been busy while we've been fighting."

Jana started going through the deleted files. Most were long scientific papers and there was a lot she didn't understand. While she was fluent in Arabic, she knew next to nothing about microbiology.

"You're going to have to help me here," Gaston said. "My Arabic is very basic. I only came to this posting three months ago."

Great. That's just great.

Jana bit her tongue. It wasn't his fault he was new.

"Here," Gaston said, pointing at one of the image files. "That's a completed culture. What does it say in the caption?"

"Marduk's Vengeance."

"Huh?"

"Marduk was a Babylonian god of war ... " Jana thought for a moment, then snapped her fingers. "I remember reading something about this. One of the Babylonian city-states didn't rebuild a temple to Marduk after it collapsed during an earthquake. The following year there was a plague that wiped out most of that city-state and several others. The ancients said that it was the vengeance of Marduk."

Gaston scrolled down until he found a string of symbols and acronyms Jana didn't understand. He read for a moment, and then let out a low whistle.

"It's a virus, and a nasty one. It looks highly contagious, with a high death rate. I've never seen a virus like this."

"That's because it probably died out three thousand years ago. The samples come from remnants of old skeletons. They stole the samples and were able to reproduce it."

"We have no modern medicine to fight this, and no natural immunity," the medic said.

Jana nodded, her mouth forming a grim line. "That's what they wanted."

Gaston kept looking at the various formulae and images while Jana translated. Her head throbbed from the battle and the confinement in this bulky suit. She ignored the pain. She had way too much to do.

She tried to stay patient while Gaston did his job, translating for him when asked. Jacob hobbled in and told them the general wasn't revealing anything, but they had learned from a villager that more than a dozen couriers had left on motorcycles several hours before.

“Damn it!” Jana cried, and instantly regretted it as pain jabbed through her skull.

“You all right?” Gaston asked.

She realized she must have flinched. “I’m fine. Keep looking.”

After a minute, the medic pointed to another image and a chemical formula.

“What’s this? Translate for me, please.”

“The Abbasid Plague. I know this one. It occurred in the late 8th century, carried by the rapidly expanding Muslim forces conquering much of the Middle East. It helped their conquest because it killed so many of the urban dwellers they set out to vanquish. It killed many in their own armies as well.”

Gaston stared at the chemical formulae and the genetic code, which he understood far better than the Arabic written on the same page.

“It’s similar to the bubonic plague but a different strain. Nasty stuff, but we can fight this with modern antibiotics. I’m surprised they’d use this.”

“They had to use what they could replicate from ancient remains. Plus, it will stoke fear. Everyone knows about the plague. It will cause panic far more than some unknown virus.”

"The death toll will surely cause panic." Gaston studied the documents for a while longer and shook his head. "Marduk's Vengeance and the Abbasid Plague are the only two they replicated. We need to send this information via satellite uplink right away."

He pulled out a thumb drive and copied everything. Then he handed it off to the unit’s communication specialist so he could run outside and transmit.

As he was doing this, Jana was checking through various documents. Much of it didn’t make sense to her, all chemical formulae and genetic codes. Since Gaston had learned so much from the tables and photos, she did an image search.

She came up with hundreds of thumbnails. She began to scroll through them, finding tables, charts, photos from archaeological sites.

Then something different caught her eye.

Two charts.

Two charts labeled “Europe” and “North America”.

Jana opened the images. She and Gaston gasped.

“Projections of the spread of the contagions,” Gaston cried.

Dr. Yasin rounded on one of the other researchers. “I told you to delete that!”

"I did!"

Gaston chuckled. "He did. But none of you deleted your files good enough."

A sick feeling spread through her stomach as she looked at the projected spread and fatalities emanating out of ten major unnamed European cities. In North America, flights would land in three unnamed international airports. The projection predicted that by the time the planes landed, everyone on board would be infected but not symptomatic. They would stay at those cities or board connecting flights and spread the diseases further.

Gaston put that on a thumb drive and Jana kept searching. She hoped to find a route for the couriers, communiques as to how they'd get across the Syrian border.

There was nothing.

She kept searching as the communications officer frantically called back to NATO, but she knew she would find no more. At least they had the target regions. Other than that, all they had was the genetic codes to two diseases that would soon be spreading in the general population, something they would have had with the first hospital admission.

General al-Rashid and Dr. Yasin were correct. Jana and her colleagues had won the battle but were at risk of losing the war.

CHAPTER TWENTY FIVE

Athens, Greece
The next day ...

Jana rubbed her gritty eyes, yawned, and studied the latest communiques. The entire world was on high alert. The border guards of every nation were thoroughly checking everyone. Some nations had locked down completely.

The speed and global nature of the response and cooperation had been impressive. The couriers carrying the disease cultures had gone in various directions. Jana had found an ereader in the secret lab that had a hidden compartment in it. Judging from this, they knew how the diseases would be smuggled. It was obvious that they would be carried in a freezer bag for as long as possible, and then the culture would be tucked in the ereader for the flight to Europe or North America.

The trick now was to find those smuggling them.

They had discovered the couriers had gone in three different routes—across the border into Iraq and then into Iraqi Kurdistan before trying to fly out to Europe, sneaking into the territory of Assad's Syrian government, and across into Turkey.

The Kurds had caught five couriers, Assad's forces had caught two, and the Turks had caught three. That left three unaccounted for.

The problem was, they had no idea which targets the three missing couriers were going for. None of the captured ones had talked, and they had all been captured before reaching the airport. None had a plane ticket on them or a passport that matched any reservations. Obviously, someone was to meet them at the airport with those things.

No country dared let down their guard.

There was another problem. Because they had warned all national governments about the fake ereaders, inevitably the press caught wind of it and spread the story around. The remaining three couriers would no doubt hear of it and hide their cultures somewhere else.

Some countries had stopped all flights. Canada had, but not the United States, saying their extra level of security would catch anyone boarding. Several European countries had stopped flights as well, and some airlines had also decided to suspend operations so as to avoid liability, but enough flights remained that there was a good chance one of the couriers would have a chance to make it to their destination as long as they could get through security.

The airports were chaos. Many travelers stayed away while others, stuck in a foreign country and needing to get home, were forced to risk flying.

With so many flights disrupted, there was a good chance one or more of the couriers would try and switch tickets at the last minute. If their flight was cancelled, they'd want to get to another target, any target, before their cultures thawed out and became active.

Of course, lots of passengers were trying to get back to Europe or North America after having flights cancelled.

Jana despaired. She and Jacob had been going through every report, every update, every communique from foreign powers who had caught one of the couriers. Hervé Boucher was back in Lebanon surveying the situation in case one tried to pass through there.

And yet, despite all this work, they had no idea where the other three couriers were or where they were headed.

***

Qa'dan al-Nimir's prayers had been answered. At least to a point. Allah was not making his martyrdom easy. The Bedouin knew he had to earn it.

General al-Rashid's second-in-command had left on a motorcycle with the other twelve couriers. Once they were out of sight of the village of Al Atlal, they split up. Some went west. Others went east. Others went north.

Qa'dan al-Nimir went north, heading to Turkey with three others. They, too, soon split up, each traveling solo.

He had gone to a town that straddled the border with Turkey. There he had shown his Turkish passport. His grandfather had been Turkish and many years ago, thinking it might be useful, Qa'dan al-Nimir had bribed a Turkish official to do some creative rewriting of the census records to make his grandfather his father. That allowed him to get a Turkish passport with a Turkish last name.

At the edge of town, he ditched the motorcycle and walked with a suitcase in one hand and the freezer bag tucked under his arm. The culture was hidden under a supply of Syrian sweets "for his family in Ankara."

He had crossed the border with no trouble, as he had many times before.

By the time he got to Ankara, things had become more complicated. His contact met him at the safehouse.

"Al Atlal was raided," his contact had told him. "They have alerted the world. Somehow the unbelievers discovered the targets are in Europe and North America. Our flight is still scheduled, but we must be extra careful."

"Our flight?"

"I am going with you. I have an EU passport, thanks to my refugee status. I can come and go as I please. But we must be careful. They will be checking every Syrian. I will go in line ahead of you and text you if I get through safely. Then you go. If I don't get through, you should abort."

"Abort? We cannot abort!"

"Then you'll have to try another way," was all his contact had told him.

They had taken separate taxis to Ankara airport. Just as they approached the outer security gate, Qa'dan al-Nimir had taken the culture out of the freezer bag, stuffed the freezer bag under the seat, and put the culture in a large camera bag. The circular plastic container for the virus culture was the identical size and shape as many of the cases for camera filters. Qa'dan al-Nimir had put two dozen filters in the bag. Slipping the frozen culture between two filters, he zipped up the bag. He had been told he would have twenty-four hours before the culture thawed. Maybe less.

It didn't matter. That was plenty of time.

Now the Bedouin stood in the departure hall. His contact had already entered security half an hour before. Ten minutes ago, he had texted 'just about to go through'.

He hadn't heard from him since.

Qa'dan al-Nimir checked his watch. Given all the delays, he would need to get in line pretty soon if he wasn't going to miss his flight. He stood on tiptoe and peered over the heads of the crowd as best he could. It looked like security was taking many people aside.

Then he realized what a stupid camouflage his camera bag was. They were sure to open it, and when they saw all the filter cases, they would immediately realize they were the same size and shape as the culture dish he was trying to hide. Then they'd notice one was cold.

He bit his lip. He was no good at this sort of thing. An honorable battle in the open was what he had always favored.

He hurried to the bathroom.

Getting into a stall, Qa'dan al-Nimir pulled out the culture and stuffed it in his pants. He winced as the cold plastic touched his shameful parts. He had endured much pain in the many battles he had fought, but nothing quite like this. With a chuckle, he zipped up his camera bag and headed for security.

It was a long wait. He did not get a text message from his contact. The man must have been pulled aside simply because he was Syrian.

The cold began to ease in his pants. The culture was thawing. He knew that once thawed, he would have only a few hours to open it, or the virus would die inside the culture dish for lack of a host cell to attach to. If he got too delayed, he would have to open up the culture in the plane and infect everyone on board.

That would mean he would die too, but then he would be in Paradise with his two sons.

Qa'dan al-Nimir smiled as he came up to the Turkish soldiers at security and handed over his Turkish passport. He eyed the full-body scanner in the other lane. If they put him through that, they'd spot the culture dish.

Luckily, they did not. It looked like they were only putting the Arabs through it.

General al-Rashid's second-in-command ended up in his seat. He sent up a prayer to Allah that he would make it to his destination in one of the great capitals of Europe. The culture would be live by then. If they tried to stop him when they landed, he would open the culture. If not, he would have just enough time to get to the release point.

And once there, the virus would spread like wildfire and nothing could stop it.

CHAPTER TWENTY SIX

Jacob grabbed his phone the instant he saw the call was from Hervé Boucher. The man had been sending regular updates via email. This was the first time he had called. That was significant.

"What you got for me?" he asked without preamble.

"Good news and perhaps a lead. It's a longshot, but it's better than nothing."

"Shoot."

"Lebanese authorities caught another courier trying to sneak across the border into Lebanon. The Lebanese used some, um, *aggressive* interrogation and the man broke. He named his partner in Beirut, who was holding his ticket and fake passport. Turns out he was flying to Bucharest."

"Romania? That's hardly a number-one target for terrorists. Wait …"

They had gathered data on the most likely targets based on the couriers they had caught. One had lived in Greece for a time and spoke Greek. Another had lived in Estonia. A third had worked as a chef in Moscow.

Those and others had all lived or worked or spoke the language of places in Eastern Europe.

Boucher read his thoughts before he could put them into words. "They're aiming for countries that don't think they'll be targets."

"You're right! They won't be as paranoid as the UK or France. Wait, and there's another reason. General al-Rashid was a pan-Arabist. He'd want to minimize Arab casualties. He gave up rather than let some Syrian kids get hurt. He won't hit Paris or London or any other city with a big Arab population. He's going to hit the smaller countries or the eastern European countries where there are hardly any immigrants. Thanks, Boucher. Thanks a million. This really helps."

"I'll call if I find out more. The Lebanese are still interrogating him but I don't think he knows any more that he's already revealed."

"They wouldn't have told him any more than he needed to know. But we got a lead now, and only two remaining couriers."

Jacob hung up. Jana had been listening in.

"We need to get everyone looking at flights to capital cities in those sorts of countries," Jana said.

They put out a message on the alert hub that the army and police of every nation looked at. Rapid communication of this kind had been unthinkable a few years ago, but with the recent unprecedented series of global attacks, mostly from Dr. Harlow and The Order, the nations of the world had set up a network to talk. Perhaps these monsters were bringing the world closer together.

After that, it was a tense hour of trawling through data, trying to find something when they didn't fully know what they were looking for.

An alert flashed over their screen. A pilot for a flight from Istanbul to JFK airport reported they had overpowered a passenger. A flight attendant had noticed a man acting suspiciously and when he went to the bathroom, gripping something inside his pocket, she had released the security catch to open the bathroom door, a feature every flight attendant but few passengers know of.

She caught the man with an open culture dish that he was just putting back in his pocket before returning to his seat.

The flight attendant turned out to have a black belt in karate and kicked the guy's ass. She and the rest of the crew tied him up, but it was too late. The culture dish was open and its contents had been circulated through the plane. Every passenger and crewman had inhaled it.

The flight was already partway across the Atlantic. It was diverted to Reykjavik and would be put in quarantine.

"Only one left," Jacob said.

"One is enough," Jana replied.

They got back to work. A minute later, they came across a report from Ankara airport. A Syrian had been detained for the simple reason that he was Syrian, and the Turks were rounding up every Syrian who tried to board a plane. He was scheduled for a flight to Doha, which didn't fit the profile, and he hadn't admitted anything, but the police said he "acted defiant."

Innocent people don't act defiant. Jacob sent a message to the Turks for more detail and then searched the flights from Ankara. They couldn't dismiss the possibility that someone was using a fake passport.

Only three flights had left Ankara heading to Europe in that timeframe. The ones going to Athens and Rome had already disembarked. Both capitals had a large Arab population. That left the final flight. It was going to Budapest, the capital of Hungary, where a conservative government had kept out most Arab immigrants.

It was the perfect target. Budapest was a popular holiday destination, and any contagion there would quickly spread.

The flight was already in the air.

Jacob alerted the aviation authorities and the Turkish and Hungarian governments. Then he called Tyler Wallace with an emergency priority to the message.

Even so, his boss only answered after a couple of minutes. The guy was seriously busy.

Jacob related everything they had discovered. Tyler Wallace replied with an offer of a private jet to Budapest.

Within five minutes, they were out the door and heading to the airport.

***

A couple of hours later, they landed at Budapest airport to find it in chaos, ringed by the flashing lights of emergency vehicles. A wide-eyed head of airport security who spoke English met their private plane.

"Someone in the central government blundered," he told them, barely able to catch his breath. "We didn't get the message in time. The flight from Ankara has already disembarked. We have locked down the airport and are pretty sure that none of the passengers had a chance to leave the building."

"Pretty sure?" Jana gasped. Her heart began to pound and that made her head pound too. "Where are the passengers now?"

"They could be anywhere. We put out a call for them, and some came to the security desk. These are the innocent ones. Others we rounded up at the baggage carousel and other places, but more than thirty are unaccounted for."

"More than thirty? That means some got out of the airport."

"Perhaps. Or perhaps they are scared to give themselves up. The army is here, and they are tromping around everywhere with assault rifles. Already, there has been an accidental shooting that killed an innocent man. A team in hazmat suits are scaring the passengers. Everyone is in a panic. We've retreated to the perimeter and the staff-only parts of the building and locked all the passengers inside."

“Wonderful,” Jana grumbled. They walked across the tarmac. They both still had their masks from the raid on Al Atlal. The head of security eyed them with open envy.

“The Turks sent us security footage of the passengers boarding the flight. We’re matching that with the passengers we’ve already accounted for and are trying to find the others. But we have more than two thousand people all over the airport. It’s going to take some time.”

The man sounded on the verge of panic. As he should be. The courier, knowing he was trapped, might decide to release the contagion in the airport. Or he might try to brave it out and see if he could escape and spread the disease somewhere that wasn’t locked down. That would be much more effective.

But soon, he would have to release the contagion, or it would die in its culture dish.

They didn’t have much time.

The security head led them to a service entrance guarded by a pair of soldiers. Once inside, they passed along some back corridors and then through a door guarded by another pair of soldiers into the main security room.

A bank of camera feeds took up one wall. The rest of the room was jam-packed with security guards, police, soldiers, and plainclothesmen who were probably from the nation's spy agency. Everyone was talking at once, and all in Hungarian, a language she did not speak. It was loud and hard to breathe. The head of security introduced them, but most of the officers there paid them little attention. All eyes were on the cameras.

“We’re not going to learn much here,” Jacob said.

“My thoughts exactly,” Jana replied. “Let’s get out among the passengers.”

Jacob tapped his mask. “We’ll stick out. They’ll know we’re from the authorities.”

Jana paused, took a deep breath, and pulled her mask off. Several people gasped and stared.

“Then we go out without them.”

Jacob pulled his own mask off and grinned. “I knew there was a reason I fell in love with you.”

They got the head of security to lead them to a door that opened onto the main terminal area. It had two policemen and two soldiers guarding it. They slipped through into a lounge area, and a hundred panicked heads turned to stare at them.

"Let's get out of here," Jana whispered.

They moved as quickly as possible down a hallway to the arrivals area. People sat on the floor or stood around, fidgeting nervously. A glum-faced family huddled in one corner, still clutching a sign that looked like it said "Welcome Home" in Hungarian, complete with smiley faces and hearts.

Jana looked around, not sure what to be looking for. Suspicious behavior? Everyone looked nervous. Many people were clustered near the exits, which had been barred and through the window she could see a line of armored police vans and more than a hundred riot police.

They walked to the baggage carousel and saw an identical scene. All airport personnel had left the main building, and they could walk where they pleased. Everywhere they went, they saw the same crowds, the same panic. They walked back to the arrivals lounge.

Then she saw him.

He was a lean, wiry man sitting against a pillar and wearing a business suit of Turkish style. He looked at Bedouin stock. Having done excavations in many remote areas across the Middle East, Jana knew the type.

What would a Bedouin be doing in Budapest?

She'd never think to ask that question except in a situation like this.

"Bedouin," she murmured, keeping her voice so low no one else would hear. "Sitting against the pillar near the vending machine."

"Got you," Jacob whispered back. "Let's take a look."

They approached at an angle to be less obvious, looking around them as they did.

When they had gotten about ten yards away, weaving between the crowd, the man looked at his watch.

As he did, Jana spotted the tattoos on his hands.

Bedouin tattoos. Specifically tattoos for a Bedouin tribe that lived in Syria.

"It's him."

Jacob didn't ask how she knew. He trusted her instinct. It was nice when a man did that.

The Bedouin looked at his watch again, got up, and began to stroll toward a nearby men's room.

"Let's do this as quietly as we can," Jacob whispered.

The man went into the men's room. Jacob followed.

Jana hesitated, cursed, and then followed too.

As she opened the door, she saw the Bedouin heading for a stall. Jacob was walking right behind him, picking up pace to gain on him. A man washing his hands at the sink glanced over at her.

He said something in Hungarian that sounded half surprised and half annoyed.

The Bedouin turned, saw Jacob bearing down on him, and saw Jana at the door.

Damn it!

Jacob lashed out. With surprising speed, the Bedouin dodged his blow, grabbed his arm, and threw Jacob against a stall door. It burst open and Jacob fell inside, making the poor man sitting on the toilet inside cry out.

Jana ran for the Bedouin, who reached into his pants and yanked out something.

Jana gasped as she saw it was a plastic culture dish.

She was almost on him. The Bedouin saw hc didn't have time, turned, and threw the culture dish as hard as he could at the wall.

Jana leaped for the culture dish, extending her body, reaching out. As she sailed through the air her fingers hit it, made it twirl in the air. She turned her body, reaching out again as she passed it by, and just managed to grab it.

She clutched it to her chest with both hands as she fell.

Her head smacked against the tile floor and all went black.

CHAPTER TWENTY SEVEN

Jana woke up to a blinding headache and Jacob's concerned face leaning over her.

She turned her head, neck and skull aching, and was surprised to see she was lying in a hospital bed.

Remembering what had happened, she changed from being surprised at waking up in a hospital to being surprised at waking up at all.

"Did we stop him?" She worried at how weak her voice sounded.

Jacob squeezed her hand. "We did. You were amazing, as usual. You should try out for the NFL. Oh, I kicked his ass for you."

"How long have I been out?"

"Only a couple of hours. They did an MRI. You have a bad concussion but no brain bleeding and no other trauma. The doctors say all you need is a week of complete rest."

Jana snorted. "That's what the last doctor said. Maybe I should listen this time."

"You can. We're done. Mission accomplished. That plane going to the States was only carrying the bubonic plague. Everyone is being treated, and there are no anticipated fatalities. We contained it."

Jana knew she should feel happy, but she did not. Picking at the edge of her blanket, she whispered, "We didn't find any connection to my father. No agents from The Order, no communiques from Dr. Harlow. Nothing."

Jacob put a hand on her shoulder. He could see the tears welling in her eyes.

"Colonel Roux said one of the general's wounded that he captured told him that al-Rashid got inspiration from the hydraulic dam attacks. When he heard that Dr. Harlow was looking for ancient technology, he got the idea of using ancient diseases. It was a copycat attack. The Order might have funded it through that fake account in Dubai, but the general thought it up all by himself."

Jana rubbed her temples, obviously in pain. "God. There will be more of these, won't there? And we still have no idea where Dad is."

Jacob hugged her. "We'll find him. I swear we will find him."

Jana could hear the doubt in his voice.

***

It had been days. Aaron Peters could not tell the passage of time more precisely than that. He knew they were deliberately messing with his sense of time. They had given him breakfast cereal when he was 99 percent sure it was dinnertime. Another time, they had given him pasta when he thought it was breakfast.

They were doing more to mess up his schedule, waking him up at random times or turning his light off only hours after he had woken up naturally. Then, for what he suspected was about three days, they hadn't turned his lights off at all.

Aaron knew the tactic. They were screwing with his head. Disorienting him. Trying to make him more susceptible to their attempted brainwashing.

The voices in his cell continued to drone on. He had come to recognize different ones, some deeper, some higher, and perhaps those of women or children. All too soft for his conscious mind to pick up.

And then there were those damn patterns that covered every square inch of his cell. Despite all those days surrounded by them, he still hadn't figured out what they depicted. Once he had worn his fingernails raw scraping the paint off several, ruining their shapes and swirls. An hour later, they took him out, drugged him, and made him watch that slideshow of the documents again. When they had returned him to his cell hours later, the patterns had been repainted.

From then on, he spent much of his time with his eyes closed.

They kept at him. Sometimes he'd be strapped to the chair and get a lecture by Tyson, or by Dr. Harlow, who always remained backlit. Sometimes they'd bring in supposed "experts" to tell him how dire the world situation was and how the best thing he could do for future generations was to join them.

He tried to tune out the lectures as much as possible. Aaron had given up arguing, given up active resistance. Now, he was in for the long haul.

Although they were right about one thing, he mused as the door slammed behind him after a particularly long lecture. The world really was going to hell in a dozen different ways, and something had to be done yesterday, not ten years from now like the current politicians put everything off. And ten years from now, they'd kick it down the road again.

Something really needed to be done. The world needed some higher, more effective power than the national governments with their shortsighted politicians and petty rivalries.

No! What am I thinking? That would end up even worse.

All that power in the hands of a few would turn them into monsters.

They already act like monsters.

Aaron lay on his blankets on the floor, closing his eyes so as not to see the patterns and pushing his fingers into his ears to block the whispering.

They always turned up the volume when he did that. It gave him a psychological edge, though. Like he was defying them.

As always, his mind worked on ways to escape. He saw none. After that one trick, they had been extra vigilant. He hadn't seen a single moment where they lowered their guard. Most of the time, Roger Tyson was on hand to add an extra level of security.

Aaron was stuck here.

Tyson …

That guy was almost as good of a fighter as he was, and backed by the guards, he could take down Aaron even if he managed to grab a gun. The Order had turned one of the greatest operatives in the world.

Only slightly less effective than I am.

That wasn't arrogance. Aaron Peters knew he was the best. The fact that his enemies had tried so hard to kill him and then finally were trying to turn him proved it.

The whispering continued, easing around the fingers he had in his ears. Even with his eyes shut, he could see the strange patterns all around his cell. His body felt strange. Nearly all his meals were drugged now. One day he had refused food and they had given him injections, so now he ate. If they were going to drug him at will, he might as well eat and keep up his strength. He'd need it if he was ever going to take on Tyson.

Between him and me, we could run this show ...

Wait. Why am I thinking that?

Why not? We'd run it better. Save the world with a strong dictatorship that wouldn't be corrupt.

Power would never corrupt me.

Damn it!

He leapt up and began to pace in his cell, shouting at the top of his lungs to drown out the insidious whispering, keeping his eyes closed to the patterns, his arms outstretched so he didn't bump in to the walls.

They were getting to him. The bastards were getting to him.

Someone turned up the volume. The voice was shouting at him now, drowning out his own cries.

No, several voices, all mixed together in a hypnotic mix that worked on his subconscious.

His legs felt wobbly. The drug was taking greater effect. Or maybe they had sprayed something through the feeding slit.

Aaron stumbled over to his bed, roll and lay down. His body felt like it was spinning. The cacophony of voices continued. For some reason, he opened his eyes. The cell's walls, ceiling, and floor danced with complex patterns.

Perhaps I could take over.

Perhaps I could run this right.

Aaron gritted his teeth, clenched his eyes shut, and started banging his head against the concrete wall.

NOW AVAILABLE!

TARGET TWELVE
(The Spy Game—Book #12)

“Thriller writing at its best... A gripping story that's hard to put down.”
--Midwest Book Review, Diane Donovan (re *Any Means Necessary*)

From #1 bestselling and USA Today bestselling author Jack Mars, author of the critically acclaimed *Luke Stone* and *Agent Zero* series (with over 5,000 five-star reviews), comes an explosive new action-packed espionage series that takes readers on a wild ride across Europe, America, and the world—perfect for fans of Dan Brown, Daniel Silva and Jack Carr.

When an artifact linked to Delphi's Oracles reveals the power to wipe clean the human mind, CIA Agent Jacob Snow and enigmatic archaeologist Jana race to prevent history's erasure. As they navigate a labyrinth of clues, they're swept into an adrenaline-fueled rush against espionage agents who are just one step away from turning leaders into tabula rasa.

An unputdownable action thriller with heart-pounding suspense and unforeseen twists, TARGET TWELVE is the twelfth novel in an exhilarating new series by a #1 bestselling author that will make you fall in love with a brand-new action hero—and keep you turning pages late into the night.

Future books in the series will soon be available.

“One of the best thrillers I have read this year. The plot is intelligent and will keep you hooked from the beginning. The author did a superb job creating a set of characters who are fully developed and very much enjoyable. I can hardly wait for the sequel.”
--Books and Movie Reviews, Roberto Mattos (re Any Means Necessary)

Jack Mars

Jack Mars is the USA Today bestselling author of the LUKE STONE thriller series, which includes seven books. He is also the author of the new FORGING OF LUKE STONE prequel series, comprising six books; of the AGENT ZERO spy thriller series, comprising twelve books; of the TROY STARK thriller series, comprising eight books; of the SPY GAME thriller series, comprising ten books; of the JAKE MERCER thriller series, comprising twenty books (and counting); of the TYLER WOLF thriller series, comprising seven books (and counting); and of the new LARA KING thriller series, comprising ten books (and counting).

Jack loves to hear from you, so please feel free to visit www.Jackmarsauthor.com to join the email list, receive a free book, receive free giveaways, connect on Facebook and Twitter, and stay in touch!

BOOKS BY JACK MARS

LARA KING THRILLER SERIES

ASSET ONE (Book #1)
ASSET TWO (Book #2)
ASSET THREE (Book #3)
ASSET FOUR (Book #4)
ASSET FIVE (Book #5)
ASSET SIX (Book #6)
ASSET SEVEN (Book #7)

TYLER WOLF THRILLER SERIES

DOUBLE AGENT (Book #1)
DOUBLE CROSS (Book #2)
DOUBLE ASSET (Book #3)
DOUBLE DOCTRINE (Book #4)
DOUBLE JEOPARDY (Book #5)
DOUBLE THREAT (Book #6)
DOUBLE TARGET (Book #7)

JAKE MERCER THRILLER SERIES

ABSOLUTE THREAT (Book #1)
ABSOLUTE DAMAGE (Book #2)
ABSOLUTE FORCE (Book #3)
ABSOLUTE PERIL (Book #4)
ABSOLUTE TREASON (Book #5)
ABSOLUTE VENGEANCE (Book #6)
ABSOLUTE TARGET (Book #7)

THE SPY GAME

TARGET ONE (Book #1)
TARGET TWO (Book #2)
TARGET THREE (Book #3)
TARGET FOUR (Book #4)
TARGET FIVE (Book #5)
TARGET SIX (Book #6)
TARGET SEVEN (Book #7)
TARGET EIGHT (Book #8)
TARGET NINE (Book #9)

TARGET TEN (Book #10)

TROY STARK THRILLER SERIES

ROGUE FORCE (Book #1)
ROGUE COMMAND (Book #2)
ROGUE TARGET (Book #3)
ROGUE MISSION (Book #4)
ROGUE SHOT (Book #5)
ROGUE STRIKE (Book #6)
ROGUE ORDER (Book #7)
ROGUE ATTACK (Book #8)

LUKE STONE THRILLER SERIES

ANY MEANS NECESSARY (Book #1)
OATH OF OFFICE (Book #2)
SITUATION ROOM (Book #3)
OPPOSE ANY FOE (Book #4)
PRESIDENT ELECT (Book #5)
OUR SACRED HONOR (Book #6)
HOUSE DIVIDED (Book #7)

FORGING OF LUKE STONE PREQUEL SERIES

PRIMARY TARGET (Book #1)
PRIMARY COMMAND (Book #2)
PRIMARY THREAT (Book #3)
PRIMARY GLORY (Book #4)
PRIMARY VALOR (Book #5)
PRIMARY DUTY (Book #6)

AN AGENT ZERO SPY THRILLER SERIES

AGENT ZERO (Book #1)
TARGET ZERO (Book #2)
HUNTING ZERO (Book #3)
TRAPPING ZERO (Book #4)
FILE ZERO (Book #5)
RECALL ZERO (Book #6)
ASSASSIN ZERO (Book #7)
DECOY ZERO (Book #8)
CHASING ZERO (Book #9)
VENGEANCE ZERO (Book #10)
ZERO ZERO (Book #11)

ABSOLUTE ZERO (Book #12)

Made in the USA
Middletown, DE
19 July 2025